Liar

from

Vermont

Liar

from

Vermont

Laura C. Stevenson

VOYAGE

Voyage
Brigantine Media
211 North Avenue
St. Johnsbury, Vermont 05819
Phone: 802-751-8802
Email: neil@brigantinemedia.com
Website: www.brigantinemedia.com

To my Vermont granddaughters
Charlotte and Madeline

Contents

Liar from Vermont...*1*

Might and Wrong...*21*

Carry Me Home...*39*

Red Letter Days...*59*

Et in Arcadia Ego...*71*

This Is the Way the Ladies Ride..............................*85*

Watersheds..*105*

Daedalus and Perdix..*125*

Femininity Quotients...*145*

Gift Horse..*163*

Liar from Vermont

The year Elizabeth II was crowned Queen of England and Edmund Hillary conquered Mount Everest, I first said I was from Vermont. To me, the three events had equal significance. No glory the Queen might have felt at Westminster Abbey could possibly have matched my pride in my identity; but the problems Hillary encountered in conquering the unvanquished peak seemed inconsequential next to the difficulties of explaining how a child born and raised near Detroit could be a native Vermonter.

My difficulties began in the suburbs of Boston two months after my seventh birthday, at Mary Anderson Memorial School. It was my first day at a public school, and I was only there for a year—the Great Man was spending two semesters at Harvard and I had to be educated in the interim. He and Mother had warned me that Mary Anderson Memorial wouldn't be at all like John Dewey Elementary, where I had gone at home. And it wasn't. We said prayers before class, just as if that were normal, and the chairs were bolted to the floor in rows, too far away from desks that were too high, so we couldn't see anybody but the teacher. The children were different, too. By nine o'clock, the yellow-shaded room was perfectly quiet while they copied the teacher's name, Miss Coffin, off the blackboard. I had never seen perfectly quiet children before—at John Dewey, we'd been encouraged to express ourselves. But Miss Coffin seemed not to notice how unnatural the silence was. She tapped up and down the aisles of studious heads, upright and immaculate in high heels, straight gray skirt, and red lipstick. My row was going to be the next-to-last she came to, I saw. Hurriedly, I wrote her name in thick pencil, then looked out the window and thought about Vermont.

"Vermont" to me was not the state, but the sagging farmhouse the Great Man had bought when I was in kindergarten. It didn't have much paint on it when we first saw it, and it had a privy instead of a bathroom. Mother had running water installed right away, and Joan, our neighbor's daughter, was so excited by the toilet that she flushed it four or five times whenever she came over. Her privy had three holes, and you washed your hands at the tap in the kitchen.

Joan's father was a farmer. He didn't talk unless he had to, but he could lift rocks onto the wall he was building for us as easily as he could boost me up on the back of Tommy, one of his roan work horses. I liked to watch him swing the boulders into place, smiling to himself while the sweat made his blue shirt stick to his back. His team helped him—patient Tommy, who looked just like him, and Teddy, who was young and not safe for kids to ride. Most of the time, they stood placidly under the apple tree, whisking their short tails at flies. But when he had loaded the stone-boat from the pile of boulders and started to back them towards it, they began to prance. I could feel the ground shake under their bucket-sized hooves from my perch, fifty feet away.

"Whoa!" They stopped, trembled, waited for him to drop the chain over the iron pin.

Clink.

They leapt forward—too soon, too soon!—"Whoa, whoa, Tommy . . ." He had to dig his heels in as they towed him forward by the reins.

"Baaaack, baaack, eeeeasy now . . ."

Foam floated out of their open mouths, and sometimes Teddy half reared, backing on his hind legs.

"Whoa." They stopped. Trembled. Waited. I dug my fingers into my hands.

Clink.

"Git!" They jumped forward together into their collars, their huge shoulders leaning over their forelegs, pulling, pulling . . . "Whoa!" Back, ever so slightly, then, "Git!" and they strained, their heads down to their knees, hooves tearing the ferns, farther, farther . . . and they were there.

"Whoa!" Teddy threw up his head and nipped at Tommy as Joan's father drove them back to the apple tree. They snorted, rubbed their faces on their legs, then began to munch grass quietly, shaking their blinders. I fed them sugar out of my trembling, flat hand, wondering at their gentleness.

"Peggy, does this look like what you saw on the board?"

Miss Coffin was standing at my right elbow, frowning. I looked at her carefully, which was how, at John Dewey, you figured out if your teacher was smarter than you were. Most of them weren't. They tended to have eyes like cows—soft and kind, but with only one expression. The Great Man said this was because they had a Theory. But there was nothing theoretical about Miss Coffin's gray-blue eyes. I decided not to sass.

"Well, no. Not exactly." The letters didn't go the same direction. They'd remarked on this at John Dewey, but they'd said it was a sign of originality.

"Let me see you write it."

I picked up the pencil in my left hand and started in as neatly as I could, but she stopped me.

"That's backwards. Can you make it go the other way?"

I could, if I really thought about it. But it was hard to concentrate with her watching like that, so some of the letters went backwards, even though the printing went the right way this time. All the other children, still silent, were watching me. I put my hand behind my back, and Miss Coffin, still frowning, finished checking the other papers in my row. I looked out the window again.

In Vermont, my hideout was across the mowing—a granite ledge, gray, streaked with white marble. At its top, moss grew thick, green, and moldy-smelling, so deep that when I lay on my back, it tickled my nose. Underneath the ledge, on its sunny side, three-leaved plants bore strawberries between the devil's paintbrushes and buttercups. Some days I lay there all morning, rolling my tongue over the tiny red sweetnesses that tasted like dirt and grass, sniffing the lemon smell of crushed fern, listening to the white-throated sparrows sing their four sad notes in the humid sunlight.

"Boys and girls," Miss Coffin was saying, "Peggy Hamilton is our new girl this year. Can you tell us a little about yourself, Peggy?"

What was there to tell? They already knew I couldn't write.

Miss Coffin smiled this time. "Just tell us what you'd like us to know about you," she prompted.

What I'd *like* them to know? Well, that was easy. "I'm from Vermont," I said proudly. "My dad has a hundred acres there, and we farm it. We have ten heifers and fifteen milk cows and a bull. And an old tractor and two work horses, Tommy and Teddy. My dad builds walls, and my mom . . . well, she helps out with the chores and stuff . . ." I stopped, my fingers crossed inside my clenched fists.

Miss Coffin looked puzzled. "Thank you, Peggy." She called a reading group to the front, and I stared at the arithmetic on the board. Slowly, I ground my first finger and thumb together as hard as I could on the top of my leg. It had been wonderful, making those quiet kids look interested. But it was a lie, and liars had to be punished.

Ω

Grammy was making sandwiches when I came home for lunch. "How was your morning, dear?"

"All right, I guess. My teacher's name is Miss Coffin."

"Poor dear! Imagine going through life with a name like that!" Grammy's name was long and German. It meant "God's chosen."

"Maybe she'll get married," I suggested helpfully. "She's pretty."

"I'm sure she will, then." Grammy spread mayonnaise over the freshly-baked bread. "Are there any nice children in your class?"

"Can't tell yet." Nice children were kids who didn't watch television or read comic books, had mothers that didn't work, and weren't either Unitarian or Catholic. They were hard to pick out on the first day of school. "Where's Mother?"

"At the faculty club with your father."

"Didn't she remember I come home for lunch here?"

Grammy's apron smelled like fresh bread as she gave me a hug. "She knew I'd be here to take care of you," she said. That was the nice thing about Grammy: taking care of me was all she had to do.

We ate our sandwiches in the dining room. There was a table in the kitchen, but civilized people didn't eat there—except in Vermont, where there was no dining room, only the kitchen, big and bright, where everybody who came to visit ended up sitting around the table. But this wasn't Vermont, so Grammy and I sat across the dining room table from each other, saying grace. That was our secret. The Great Man didn't believe in God, and at John Dewey they said He was optional, but He was a private friend of Grammy's and mine. Sometimes we read the

Bible together, when my parents were out. Grammy knew all the best stories.

"Grammy," I said after we'd finished, "don't you wish we'd moved to Vermont instead of here?" In Vermont, nobody cared which way my printing went.

"Vermont is nice in the summer," she said, "but you'd get tired of eating in the kitchen and using paper napkins if we did it all year around."

I liked paper napkins, but I knew it was useless to argue. "Yes, but wouldn't it be wonderful to have our own cows, so we could milk them and drink it all warm, right out of the pail?"

"Gracious! Can you imagine me milking a cow?" She was sitting with her back to the window, and the light behind her caught the white hairs that had slipped out of her bun, making her a delicate halo. The hands folded on her placemat were so thin I could see all the little bones that became her fingers where her palms stopped being palms. No, I couldn't imagine her milking a cow, much less doing the other chores I knew had to be done when you kept cows in a barn.

"Well, I'd milk the cows, then. You could make bread and watch sunsets."

Grammy laughed. "It would be too cold to watch sunsets in winter, dear." But as she cleared the plates, I knew she was thinking about Vermont evenings, when she sat on the stone slabs that made the front steps of our house, watching the sun lower itself into the purple gray mountains and the faraway mirror of the lake. After it was gone, the clouds blazed pink and orange, and Grammy, facing them, became a pastel reflection of their softness—serene, remote, untouched by the world.

"Peggy?" Grammy's hand patted my shoulder. "The police-woman has come on duty, and here you are, just sitting and dreaming. You'd better hurry."

I hurried, wondering how I was ever going to be able to

explain to the other kids that I lived in Vermont, when they could see I lived right across the street from school.

It turned out not to be a problem; the kids never put two and two together. That made them different from my friends at John Dewey, who would have seen through my fibs in two seconds, beaten me up, and then wanted to learn all about the farm. I was glad not to be beaten up, though I knew peer pressure was an important factor in developing a conscience. On the other hand, since everybody believed me, I had to go on lying, and that got harder and harder. Lying to Miss Coffin, for instance, was so tough—she always paid attention to details, and sometimes I forgot which ones I'd added—I didn't see how I could keep it up for two whole terms. And then there was Mr. Kerry, the principal. Every time it was my turn to take a note to the office, he'd put his head out of his special little room and say, "How's the little girl from Vermont?" So to keep up face, I'd have to tell him how the cows were doing, or later in the fall, how we were splitting wood for the stoves— "It's hard, Mr. Kerry. You have to hit the log in exactly the right place, or your maul just bounces back."

"Yeah? What's a maul, Peggy?"

He sure didn't know much about farming. "It's like a sledge-hammer, only one end is like an ax. You use the ax end to split logs, and the hammer side makes it heavier."

"You don't say!" His eyes were large and brown, and he liked to listen to me. Probably he had a Theory. Sometimes he walked me back to my classroom, his white socks flashing between his pants and his shoes. When I got to my seat, I'd pinch myself once for each time I'd fibbed to him. The whole top of my left leg was purple, now, and I'd had to start in on the right one. When the nurse who did the physicals asked me how on earth I'd gotten all those bruises on my thighs, I said I'd run into a hedge on my bike. I gave myself two pinches for that later on—one about the hedge, and the other because I didn't have a bike.

A week after the physicals, Miss Coffin gave me a sealed envelope to take home.

"What's in it?" I asked with John Dewey suspicion.

"A note about a conference that I'd like to have with your mother." Her voice told me John Dewey suspicion didn't sit very well with her, but I didn't take the note, even so.

"Is it about my printing?" Miss Coffin had noticed I threw a ball with my right hand, so she'd suggested I try writing with that hand, too. My right hand didn't know any more about making letters than my left knew about throwing balls, but Miss Coffin said it would learn if I practiced. It didn't. After six weeks, I still picked up the pencil in my left hand unless she stopped me, and no matter how hard I tried, the letters wouldn't stay on the lines.

"That, and a few other things."

"Mother's pretty busy with the faculty women's cl—" oops— "I mean, the Farm Bureau. They really need women to help work for government subsidies, so she doesn't have much time."

Miss Coffin smiled a little smile I didn't like very much and pushed the note into my hand. "I'm sure we can arrange a time when she can see me, Peggy."

I was sure, too. Miss Coffin never had trouble getting what she wanted. I scuffed my shoes as hard as I could on the sidewalk as I dawdled past the statue of Mary Anderson. It was all going to come out now—and what would Grammy say when she found out I was a liar? Would she let God forgive me? Maybe He would forgive me even if she didn't, but what good would that do? And what if He turned out to be optional after all?

When I got home, Grammy and Mother were setting the table with the best china and silver.

"Who's coming?" I asked. "Can I eat with you?"

"*May* I," said Mother, giving me a hug. "It's a special party to celebrate your father's translation of *The Odyssey*."

I liked *The Odyssey*. The Great Man had read bits of it to

me as he translated along. The stories in it were cool—every bit as gory as the ones in the Bible. "Can . . . may I help you get things ready?"

"Grammy and I can do it faster by ourselves, dear."

"I wish Pris were home." Pris was my next older sister. She went to Radcliffe. Our oldest sister, Liz, had graduated and gotten married.

"We all miss Pris, but she's having a good time on her own, isn't she?"

"Grammy, will you read me a story?"

"Not right now, dear."

As I started upstairs, I remembered the letter. "Oh, Mother! Miss Coffin sent you a note." She put it in her apron pocket, which might or might not be a good sign.

I went to my room and drew a picture of a white farmhouse on a hill. In back of it, I drew a purple line for mountains, and just on top of them I set a big orange-red sun. Carefully, I began to color the sky light pink at the bottom, and darker in the middle, and finally blue at the top. As I added a few dark clouds, I suddenly stopped. I was holding the crayon in my left hand. I looked at my farmhouse, perched peacefully on its green-gray hill. Two small tears spattered down on the page, smearing the sunset. I went into the bathroom, got a Kleenex, and tenderly blotted them off.

Ω

At quarter to seven, I was dressed in the blue smocked dress Grammy had made me, and sitting on Mother's bed, watching her screw her earrings tightly onto her ears.

"How come you don't get your ears pierced?" I asked.

"Good heavens, dear! Where did you get such a bohemian idea?"

Bohemian ideas seemed not to be good ones, so rather than get Pris in trouble by saying I'd gotten it from her, I changed the subject. "Can we go up to Vermont next weekend?"

"Possibly," she said. "That will be about the last time until next spring."

"The last time!"

"You forget," she said, "it's going to snow up there soon, and they don't plow the road to our house. We'll just shut it down for the winter, the way we do when we're in Michigan."

"Do you suppose it misses us when we're gone?"

Her reflection gave mine a gently reproving smile. "Do you *really* think a house can miss people?"

Did I *really* . . . ? I thought of coming in on weekends, sniffing the damp smell of unheated house as I hurried through the kitchen where the china lay behind glass doors, waiting to be used on the table that stood waiting to be set. Of running up the steep stairs to my room to find the old jeans and sweaters I wore in Vermont and nowhere else. Of hugging the chilly stuffed animals who had been waiting patiently for me to take them out of their silent rows. Thoughts like that made it hard to say houses couldn't miss people, though even I knew that was supposed to be the truth. But rather than risk lying any more, I said, "Well, *I* miss it—all the time."

"I know you do." Mother sighed, and I waited for her to remind me Harvard was Important in a way Vermont somehow wasn't—but she was absorbed in placing her silver combs behind her ears, making her hair puff out over her earrings.

"Mommy, you're so pretty."

"Why, thank you, Peggy." She turned around and smiled, a smile like Grammy's, from deep inside her eyes. When she smiled like that, she looked very fragile, and younger than I was. "Shall we do your braids?"

I sat in front of the mirror and watched her hands part my

hair into scraggly blond strands. "Your bangs are crooked, aren't they?" she said. "Shall I . . . ?"

"People will be here before you're done," I said quickly. My hair was straight and fine, and when she tried to even my bangs out, they slipped away from her scissors until they were so short they stuck out in a little fringe.

"All right." She glanced at the clock and braided fast, pulling the little wispies that grew down my neck. "There!" she said, dissatisfied. They were already beginning to slip out, but there was no time to fix them, let alone ask her about Miss Coffin's note, even if I had dared. The doorbell was ringing.

Dinner was served at eight. The guests were arranged boy-girl-boy-girl around the table ("so the men won't just talk to each other"), down to the corner where I sat on Mother's left. There were lots of people there. The man next to Grammy was Mr. Steiner, a psychologist— "one of those people who think everything we do has to do with sex," Mother had explained earlier. One could only pity him. In our family, man was a rational creature, and sex was what dogs did. Then there were some people from the Classics Department, who all looked alike, even their wives, and Mr. Zander. Mr. Zander taught English. He wrote novels instead of real books, but they must have been pretty good, because the Great Man said it wasn't every day young writers got tenure at Harvard. The important thing about him, though, was that he had a summer place in Vermont, and we had been staying with him there when he'd persuaded the Great Man to buy ours. Ever since then he'd been my special friend, and tonight he was sitting next to me. He was wearing a blue tie with bulldogs on it, and some words on little shields. I stared at the letters as the Great Man carved the roast.

Mr. Zander smiled. "Can you read yet, Peggy?"

"Sure. I'm in the Highest Group."

"Well, can you read this?" He held out the tie so I could see it better.

I spelled it out carefully. "The first word is lux. Then et. Then veri . . . veritas."

"Good for you," he said, his blue eyes crinkling behind his glasses. "Do you know what it means?"

All the guests were smiling as they waited for me to admit that I didn't, but I could do a little better than that. "It's Latin," I said. "And *veritas* is on all the notebooks here, so it must have something to do with Harvard."

"You're absolutely right, my little classicist," he said. "It means *truth*, which Harvard purports to value. But this is Yale, which also values *lux*. Which means . . . ?"

"Well," I hazarded, "it sounds like *luck*, but—"

"—Luck and Truth!" he said, delighted. "Marvelous!"

Everybody laughed, and I joined in, but I didn't really feel like it. If truth was as big a deal at Harvard and Yale as it was in the Bible, luck wasn't going to do me much good. I looked down at my napkin.

In my hideout, thick green moss grew over the top, but next to that was a brown, thinner kind that had fairy cups sprouting out of it after it rained. Then there was a taller, leafier kind that smelled like mint when you crushed it, and finally a ground-pine that looked like cactus—or might, if you were very small. I weeded around it and made a little track through it. Hundreds of ants passed back and forth on my track, carrying white eggs in their mouths. I wondered if they thought they were in a desert.

Mr. Zander's hand fell on my shoulder. "Hey!" he whispered. "Come back to us!"

"See?" Mother was saying in the bright tone she used when she pretended nothing was wrong, "She just slips away."

"Well, she comes by it honestly," said Mr. Zander, smiling as he looked down the table to the Great Man's abstracted face.

"Where do you go when you slip away, Peggy?"

"Vermont." Where else would anyone go?

He kissed me on the forehead, which sort of surprised me. "Vermont," he said. "*Veritas* indeed—and not on a notebook, either. You're a discerning child."

"She's more than that," Mother said, sighing. "I just got a note from her school, saying she's been telling everyone that Edward is a farmer and we live in Vermont. Not just the children—her teacher, and even the principal!"

I stole a glance at Grammy, but she looked busy with her roll, and maybe she really was. She didn't hear very well when lots of people were talking at once. Next to her, though, Mr. Steiner stopped looking bored and stared at me through his funny glasses, and the Classics wife on his far side seemed to be interested, too.

In Vermont, I thought desperately, there's a Model A in the barn cellar. It's rusted apart, but you can still open the door . . . it was no good. Everybody was looking at me now, so I knew I was going to be The Subject of Discussion. That was what happened in our family when you did something terrible, unless the Great Man noticed—in which case he roared at you, and you cried and stopped doing it. Generally, though, it was women who noticed terribleness, and since it was unbecoming for women to raise their voices, we handled things this way.

Because there were so many people, the Discussion was quite lively and a little hard to follow. From what I could gather, the school had said that lying could imply a serious emotional disturbance, which some people said was the case and others said was the kind of cant you got from schools these days. Then there was some stuff about guilt and self-punishment that made me wonder who had told Mother I was pinching myself, but I never found out, because Mr. Steiner was talking loudly about a dreadful condition that started with "skits" and had something to do with dreaming off. Meanwhile, people were passing heaped-up plates to each other—all the way around the table, the way they always seemed to—and filling each others' glasses, and by the time everybody was served, the only clear result was that as these things went, I was getting off lightly. The guests, though interested in my condition, seemed unconcerned by the depths of my depravity; the Great Man hadn't been paying attention; and Grammy had drifted off to someplace of her own where there was no loud laughing or smoking or drinking.

During the next few minutes, there was nothing but the hungry clanks of forks—no wonder, since it was 8:30 by now—interspersed with comments on how good everything was. Then one of the Classicists started talking about Stalin, Mrs. Steiner started talking about her exotic new hairdresser, and a bunch of little conversations started up. Just as I began to feel safe, I heard Mr. Zander say quietly, "Do you have any idea what you've done?"

When I turned to see who he was talking to, I saw he was looking at me with the kind of pitying smile you give to sinners before you shape them up. Well, I deserved it, but I felt a stab of betrayal. As a veteran Subject of Discussion, I knew there were some people who just *had* to add a little lecture of their own after everything was over. But it hurt to think that Mr. Zander, third in line after God and Grammy, was one of them. The food on my plate blurred as I looked down at it.

"That's what I was afraid of," he said softly, handing me his handkerchief. "Listen, Peggy. Don't let them get you down. You've pulled off a magnificent feat."

I stared at him over the perfect white folds. "I what?"

"You've done something extraordinary."

"I *have?*"

"Shh," he said, glancing around the table. "You'll start them off again. But yes. You've told a story that has held the attention of a whole school for six weeks. That's just—amazing."

The way my mouth dropped open would have made him think I was a total retard if the Classics wife on his right hadn't rescued me by asking him a question about Stalin. As it was, I had time to pull myself together before he turned back to me.

"Now then," he said—softly again— "as I was saying, you're a wonder."

Maybe I wasn't as together as I thought. "But didn't you understand . . . ?"

"I understood enough to realize you told a fantastic story."

"But it wasn't *true*," I said. "It was a lie. Like . . . like Stalin. And look—didn't he die? I thought it was a big deal—"

"—Yes, he died, and yes, it was a big deal, but no, what you told was *not* a lie like Stalin. It was a lie like . . . Odysseus."

"Odysseus? *He* was a liar?"

"A consummate liar. Of the highest order." He smiled at my shocked face. "Last time you and I talked about Odysseus, we were watching your family play croquet, and you were telling me the story of the Cyclops. Do you remember?"

I nodded. Of course I remembered. The sun had been just about ready to go down, the hermit thrushes had been singing in the woods, and the swallows had been racing over the mowing, diving and snapping at the last bugs of the evening.

"We didn't mention who tells that story in the poem—but do you know?"

"Sure. Odysseus tells it to a bunch of people at a dinner party."

"That's my girl," said Mr. Zander. "Now, tell me. Do you think the people at the dinner party believed the story?"

My eyes opened wide. "You mean, they didn't?"

"Well, let's see," he said. "Believing it involves believing that Odysseus and his men sailed to an island inhabited by many giants but met only one, that the one was so big that he could pick up two men, smash them together and eat them raw in a couple of mouthfuls, that he spoke fluent Greek, that there was a log lying in the cave right where Odysseus needed it . . ."

"But if they had said those things, they would have wrecked the story!"

"So you're saying they didn't believe the details, but they believed in the story-ness of the story and they admired the skill of the man telling it?"

That seemed to be what he wanted me to have said, so while it was a lot more complicated than anything I could have come up with on my own, I said yes.

He smiled. "Fine. Now tell me—does everybody in your school *really* believe you live on a Vermont farm?"

"I . . ." Come to think of it, did they? They seemed to, but . . . "I don't know."

"C'mon, Peggy. It's a public school, right?"

"What's that have to do with it?"

"Everything. A public school is supported by town taxes, so it's open only to kids who live in the town."

"That sounds fair," I began judiciously—then I saw what he was driving at. "You mean I couldn't go to Mary Anderson Memorial if we didn't live here?"

"Right. Now, most of your classmates, and certainly your teacher and your principal, know that. And yet—well, you tell me. When you talk about the way you live on 'your' farm in Vermont, what do they do? Call you a liar? Walk away?"

"No. They listen."

"And why would they do that?"

"Because . . ." I thought of Mr. Kerry's face, and even, sometimes, Miss Coffin's. "Because they're . . . interested."

"You bet they are. This is undoubtedly the first time any of them have met a second-grader who can make life on a Vermont farm as real to them as Odysseus made the Cyclops real to the people at the dinner party."

There was something he was missing. I couldn't quite figure out what it was, but it seemed so important that I objected instead of just shutting up. "Um . . . the life they're listening to isn't *mine*," I said. "It's sort of Joan's but not really. It's the life I . . . er . . . go to, like I did when you—"

"—Called you back?" He smiled as he took his handkerchief, but his eyes were serious. "Sure. That's why you can tell such a convincing story."

"But isn't going to a place like that . . . isn't that wrong? I mean, I *know* it's not real, but sometimes it's so much realer than . . ." I looked around the table. "Well, this. Or school. Isn't that skits o . . . whatever Mr. Steiner was saying?"

"No, no," he said, glancing anxiously across the table. "It's doing what you have to do when you don't quite fit into the puzzle you've got to live in. Unfortunately, the experts who classify the pieces of modern puzzles tend to think that a kid who can share her imaginary life in a way that makes her auditors hear a higher truth has something wr—" He broke off, his face a sudden mask of politeness as he looked past me at Mother. "Splendid dinner, Ellen," he said. "Absolutely perfect for the occasion."

"Oh, thank you!" she said, and I knew she was really pleased, because he was a fussy eater—only with adults, you had to call it a gourmet—and she'd been worried about cooking something he'd enjoy. "What are you two talking about so seriously?"

"The Vermont we have in common," he said. "And I was just about to suggest that Peggy write down some of her daydreams for other people to read."

"Oh, she can't," said Mother, quickly, ashamed. "We've just learned that her penmanship skills are way below grade level. I'm sure the problem is temporary, but . . ."

Mr. Zander looked from her to me. "A smart girl like you has trouble writing?"

"Only with my right hand," I said. "My left hand writes okay, except sometimes it goes backwards. That's wrong, so at school I have to write with the hand you're supposed to write with—"

"—What!?" said Mr. Steiner, Mr. Zander, and Mother, almost at the same time. The next moment, Mother was asking me reproachfully why I hadn't *told* her, and everyone else was agreeing that making left-handed people write with their right hands was a holdover from the Victorians, who seemed to be right up there with the bohemians when it came to bad ideas. In the middle of the noise, the Great Man began to speak, and as usual when he had something to say, everybody hushed. He paused to light a cigarette, then gave me a benign smile from his end of the table. "Peggy," he said, "did you tell your teacher you can type?"

I shook my head. "It . . . it didn't seem to be the issue."

"Not the issue?" he said. I knew something was coming, because he was using the tone that meant he and I were secret conspirators against Rules, Women, or Theories, depending. Even so, I was dumbfounded when he began to explain—to everybody, now—that when he'd seen me writing backwards, he'd decided to try teaching me to type, to see if that would help me get used to seeing the way words were supposed to appear on the page. It was news to me that he knew I was left-handed, let alone that I wrote backwards. As for the lessons, I knew that if you wanted his attention you had to do something with him that he enjoyed, like typing, and you had to catch on fast or he got bored—but I had never dreamed I'd been helping him work out an educational idea. That was nifty, especially when he wound up by giving Mother the modest smile that meant he knew he was right. "Maybe you should talk to that teacher of hers, Ellen," he said. "Tell her Peggy uses all the right fingers, and she can do around forty words a minute copying—less, of course, if she has to think up spelling for herself."

A murmur of admiration went around the table, and as I

began to clear the plates, one of the Classicists said how smart it was to see past the problem of penmanship into the problem of written communication. That gave the Great Man an opportunity to say that typing helped with spelling too, because your fingers memorized the pattern of the letters, and everybody (including me) saw right away how true that was. By the time Mother had served up Grammy's special angel food cake, everybody was saying what a brilliant teacher the Great Man was, and that turned into talk about his wonderful new translation, with lots of readings from the advance copy of his new book, which I fetched from his study after carefully washing my hands. Then there were speeches and toasts in champagne for the guests and sparkling grape juice for Grammy and me, and finally, the guests went into the living room for coffee, which was my signal to say good night politely and to go upstairs.

I always approached the moment nervously, because while it usually just drew comments on how well brought up I was, sometimes one of the ladies (or worse, one of the old men) asked for a kiss good night, and then, of course, everybody else had to show they liked children, too, and I had to deliver kisses all round. Tonight, though, there were so many people and conversations that only Grammy said good night back, and I slipped upstairs without any comments at all.

It was cool and quiet in my room, and I undressed by the light of the street lamp outside. The voices from the party drifted into the bathroom as I brushed my teeth, and one of them was Mr. Zander's, talking quietly about a poor kid who was going to have a tough life. I listened a little more, but the only thing that floated upstairs was cigarette smoke, so I closed my door and crawled under my blankets.

You were supposed to be good to the unfortunate people in the world, so I said a special prayer for the kid who was going to have a tough life. Then for a little while, I thought about Odysseus and puzzles, but I was too sleepy to figure it all out. Pulling my pillow over my head, I left Miss Coffin, Mary Anderson, and luck and truth all behind me, and slowly slipped into the real world, where I lay on a bed of green moss, sniffing the lemon smell of a crushed fern and listening to a white-throated sparrow sing its four sad notes in the humid sunlight.

Might and Wrong

The summer I turned eight, Erma Oldcastle got a horse. His name was Prince, and he caused considerable awkwardness in my family, because I *hadn't* gotten a horse—and not for want of asking, either. I'd begged for one. I'd prayed for one. Every birthday and every Christmas I had run downstairs early in the morning, hoping to find that my parents had secretly delivered a horse in the night, the way parents often did in books. They hadn't, and the explanation was always the same. Horses were expensive. Only people with Real Money could afford to own them. Everybody—the Great Man, Mother, Grammy, and even my grownup sister Pris, who had wanted a horse herself before Harvard men had redirected her attentions—said so.

But here was Prince, with his white star and kind eyes. And he belonged to Erma Oldcastle, whose family had no money, real or otherwise. They lived a quarter of a mile away from us, across the road from a barn that rose so high that it felt like a church when you stood in its big door and looked up through musty cracks of sunlight to the rafters. If you turned around in that doorway, you looked slap into the house, because all that separated it from the road was some packed dirt crowded with old trucks, farm machinery, and hounds. The hounds lived under the front porch, which was up a flight of steps because the house was built into the side of a hill. Once upon a time it had been as grand as the barn, but now the steps were rotting, the fancy railings were falling off, and the porch listed towards the road, weighed down by a refrigerator, laundry that never seemed to dry, a couch, and Mrs. Oldcastle, who spent a lot of time sitting there and yelling at Erma and Avery.

All that yelling made you sorry for Erma, who had a shy smile and eyes as brown and kind as Prince's. But Avery . . . well, you had to admit he deserved it. He wasn't just obnoxious, like some of the boys in school. He was scary. Take the time he showed up when Rob and Joan came over with Mr. Bartlett to split firewood. Joan wrinkled her nose (he was so dirty he smelled), but Mr. Bartlett threw her a look and said he could stay if he helped. The moment Mr. Bartlett turned his back, Avery climbed a tree—and a few minutes later, when a plane went overhead, he jumped down on top of Joan and me, yelling "Git down! Git down! A bomber's gonna git us!" He practically smothered us, but I still had breath enough to be shaking, and Joan was screaming—then Mr. Bartlett strode over and pulled him off us, gave him a shake, and told us there were no bombers, Avery was just fooling. When we started stacking again, Avery grinned at Rob and said something about boys having hot dogs and girls having banana splits. Instead of laughing, Rob turned red, and Mr. Bartlett whirled around and told Avery to git lost. He didn't raise his voice, but all of us shivered, and Avery slunk off and stayed gone for the rest of the summer.

But the first time Erma rode Prince past our house, there was Avery up behind her. And true to form, instead of just sitting there when I went running out to say hi, he slid off and pointed to our porch. "Lookit them damn birds nestin' on your light!"

What he was talking about was our phoebes. They'd made a nest on the porch light right after we'd put it in our first summer, and they'd come back every year after that. They were half tame, and we got really fond of them. The whole time they were sitting on their eggs and raising their fledglings, we didn't flick on the light, and when they left in late summer, it was always kind of sad.

"Avery," I began, "Those birds are—"

"—Shitheads!" he said, starting down the driveway. "Jist lookit your porch! I'll fix *them*, fast enough!" He picked up a long stick.

"Avery!" said Erma, her eyes wide.

Her voice hardly carried, and I knew yelling was all Avery paid attention to, so I took off after him as fast as I could without spooking Prince. "Avery! Cut it out! We *like* those birds!"

It was hopeless, of course. He jumped up on the porch, swinging his stick at the mother phoebe as she darted away from the nest. I was close enough now to grab for Avery's stick, but he was sure to hit *me* with it if I missed, so the nest would've been a goner if Grammy hadn't hurried out the door, looking like the wrath of God in an apron dusted with flour.

"What are you *doing*?" she said in a voice I had never heard her use before.

Avery lowered his stick. "Gittin' rid of them birds for you," he said to the floor. "I do it all the time at home."

"This isn't your home, is it?"

I knew enough about Avery's foul mouth to hold my breath, but he just said, "Nope."

"Then leave our phoebes alone," she said. She looked past him at Erma, who had ridden Prince up the driveway and halted him in the yard. "What a nice horse," she said stepping out the door in a way that made Avery back off the porch. "Peggy, why don't you find him a carrot?"

I scooted in and out quickly, and when I reached the yard again, I was surprised to see Grammy patting Prince. "My father had a bay that looked like this," she was saying to Erma. "He seems nice and quiet."

Sometimes you remembered that when Grammy was a kid, there were no cars or tractors, and even people who were a little afraid of horses knew something about them.

Erma nodded. "He's real good. Never acts up, even when you ride him double."

I gave Prince the carrot and stroked his soft nose, knowing there was no hope at all that Erma could offer me a ride. Grammy was being perfectly nice, but Erma's wide, pretty face told me she knew they weren't welcome, and even Avery was standing still.

"He certainly is handsome," said Grammy. "Where did you find him?"

Erma hesitated, so Avery butted in. "Dad won him off Joe the Frenchman. Royal flush."

For a moment I thought a royal flush had something to do with toilets, but Grammy's little intake of breath cleared me up.

"Gracious!" she said. "Well, you two enjoy your ride, now." She took my hand. "I'm sure Peggy will envy you."

She stepped back, gently pulling me with her. Erma reached down; Avery grabbed her arm, jumped up behind her, and they rode out the driveway without a word. The father phoebe stationed himself on a fence post across the road, his tail bouncing as he watched them go.

Ω

"So," said the Great Man at lunch. "Your friend Erma has a horse and you don't—is that what you're going to say?"

I knew plenty better than to say it. "Erma's nice, but she isn't my friend," I said. "Thirteen's too much older than me."

"Well, that's true," he admitted. "And she's getting pretty, poor girl." He glanced at Mother and shook his head. "Not much hope—" He broke off as a truck pulled up in the driveway.

"Hey, it's Weller," he said with a big smile. "Stick around for the good time."

I stuck, because Mr. Weller was interesting. He always wore overalls, a green-gray shirt, rubber boots, and a canvas hat, and he didn't shave very often, so you'd think he was one of the men who leaned against the old bank downtown, chawing, spitting, and collecting news. But he wasn't. He owned the barn across from Oldcastles', plus their house, both parts of what the Great Man called his "spread"—650 acres, four barns, two sugar houses, a sawmill, a herd of milking cows, fifteen heifers, and a pasture full of beef cattle. Three men worked for him, big and friendly, except Mr. Oldcastle, who was thin and looked at you in a way that made you feel uncomfortable.

Mr. Weller heaved himself onto the porch, frightening the phoebes. The Great Man offered him a chair, and Mother offered him coffee, but he turned them both down. "Can't stay," he said. "Gotta get the hay in. Just thought I'd check to see if you'd had a visit from the tax man that's been snoopin' around."

The Great Man looked interested. "This area's being reassessed?"

"Nope. That happened five years back. This fellow's different. Young, suit and tie, little badge, briefcase—the US government."

I thought back to the car that had crept by when I'd been watching the phoebes and feeling bad about not being able to ride Prince. "Does he drive a blue car like he's not sure he's on a road?"

"You got it," he said, grinning. "Real city boy. Stopped when he got to the Oldcastles', thinkin' it was a dead end. Lucky I was there." He looked conspiratorially at the Great Man. "See, the folks in Washington think I should pay taxes."

"Of course!" said Mother. "Everybody pays taxes!"

"Everybody pays *some* taxes," corrected Mr. Weller. "Like the ones that go to the school, the roads, the fire house, and such.

I got no quarrel with that, though you may have heard different down street. See, they overcharged me considerable on the place Oldcastles live in. 'Valuable house,' they say. 'Belonged to Judge Beecher.' 'Beecher's fifty years gone,' I say. 'Take a look at his house *now* before you say what it's worth.' 'Okay, okay,' they say. 'We'll do an assessment.' So I'm waitin', that's all. But when it comes to the US government, I draw the line. Socialists, the whole lot of them. Take money from workin' men and give it to the shiftless. Terrible."

I glanced at Mother. She was chairman of the Democratic Women's Club, and Democrats didn't say things like that. But she just smiled and asked, "How do you get around paying taxes?"

"Easy," he said. "They're *income* taxes, and I got no income." He shifted himself against the door frame; I heard the phoebes flutter anxiously. "I sell milk, but I gotta hire help gettin' it in. I got tenants, but I gotta keep their places up. It's all on paper in that barn across from Oldcastles', an' the youngster sees the proof when he looks over the books. Then he turns to sugarin'. An' for a moment, I'm worried." He looked at the Great Man. "Now, you know how it is, Professor Hamilton. A man's gotta make money *somewhere*, and between my sugarbush and the one you so kindly let me use, I had both sugar houses goin' most of March and some of April this year."

"So you made a profit!" said the Great Man. "How unfortunate."

"Yep. *An'* unfortunate that I'd stored all them cans in the barn, set for the Vermont Gifts place down street. 'Course I think of applyin' persuasion, since there's four of us there, unloadin' the hay. But first I decide to try somethin'. I say, 'What makes you think I sell it? You got any receipts there?'

"'Well, no," he says, looking addled. "'But here it is, ready to be shipped.'

"'Oh no,' I say, lookin' round at Oldcastle, Crawford, and

Wolfson. 'I don't sell it. I pour it on the hay—one quart every five bales. Makes the cows give sweeter milk.'

"Wal, Oldcastle lets out that bark he makes instead of laughing, but Crawford, smooth as syrup he says, 'Sometimes, it's gotta be a quart for every *four* bales. It's a sacrifice, but ask around—Weller's milk is sweeter than anybody else's.'" Mr. Weller's eyes sparkled ice gray. "And would you believe it, Professor Hamilton, that city slicker wrote off a two thousand dollar loss, got into his car and drove away with all Oldcastle's hounds bayin' at him!"

"Wonderful!" said the Great Man. And we laughed until Mr. Weller turned to me.

"You seen Erma's hoss?"

I nodded. "She rode him by today. He's beautiful."

"Sure is," he said. "Well-trained, too. Never should have fallen into those hands."

Mother looked uncomfortable. "Oh, I'm sure Erma takes good care of him."

"She sure does!" I said. "He's just *shining!*"

Mr. Weller shrugged as well as he could against the door frame. "She's earned him, for sure," he said. "Folks say her old man—wal, folks say a lot. But if they say a family that can't get its rent together has no call to own a $500 ridin' hoss . . . I gotta agree."

The Great Man pulled reflectively on his cigarette. "Oldcastle owes you rent as well as work?"

"He warn't supposed to," said Mr. Weller. "Deal was, he'd live in the ol' Beecher place free if he fixed it up. That was three years ago, and the sonofa—excuse me, ladies—hasn't so much as lifted a hammer. So last March I told him he owed me three years of rent, and he said he'd get it by May, for sure. But with him, 'for sure' means he's layin' his paycheck against a good hand—happen you know the type."

Grammy shook her head, but the Great Man nodded. "So he owes you the horse?"

"Depends on who you ask. *He* says, give him time, he's got more to work with now. *I* say all I gotta do is go to court . . . but, see, the girl likes it. Makes it hard to do what I should." Suddenly he looked at me. "Say, don't you need a hoss, Peggy? This one would be perfect for you. Quiet, no vices—he'd take you any place you wanted to go."

I held my breath, because instead of saying the usual things about owning a horse, the Great Man looked at Mother. "You know, if Erma could take care of him for the winter . . ."

Mr. Weller coughed. "I expect the Oldcastles will've moved on by then."

"Ah," said the Great Man.

The kitchen was so quiet you could hear the rustlings of the birds outside, then a shrill squeak. Mr. Weller looked over his shoulder. "Seems *you* got tenant problems."

"Oh, those are just the phoebes," said Mother. "We like them."

"Too bad," said Mr. Weller. "See out there? Those'r tree swallows fixin' to move in."

I ran to the window just in time to see a strange bird sweep onto the porch. There was a terrific rustling and squawking, and the father phoebe flew out with the stranger darting after him. Out over the yard, another swallow joined it, and they dive-bombed him. He swooped and fought, but they were faster and stronger, and there were two of them. After a minute, one of them saw an opening and dove right at his head. There was a terrible shriek; then he started to flutter, and both of them attacked him at once.

I raced towards the door, but Mr. Weller stopped me. "Best not go out there," he said, not unkindly. "It ain't gonna be pretty."

"But somebody has to stop them!" I said. "They're pecking out his eyes!"

"That's what they do."

"But the phoebes were here first! It's not fair!"

"It's fair if you're a swallow."

I looked desperately at Mother, Grammy, and the Great Man, but they were all staring out the window, their faces frozen in horror. Looking out myself, I saw the father phoebe crash into one of the Adirondack chairs and thump to the ground, while the swallows started in on the mother.

Mr. Weller pushed himself off the doorframe. "Tell you what," he said. "On my way out, I'll wave my hat. That'll stop 'em for awhile—No, don't bother," he added as Mother began to get up. "Be seein' you soon."

He left, and through the window I could see him flapping his hat. It worked—the swallows went one way and the mother phoebe went the other. But she was flying strangely, and the father phoebe didn't get up, even when the truck drove off.

"Dreadful," muttered the Great Man, his hands shaking as he lit a cigarette. "Horrible. Nature red in tooth and claw." He looked out the window once more, then started towards his study.

I inched towards the door.

"Peggy!" said Mother. "Don't go out there!"

"But—"

The Great Man spun around. "YOU HEARD YOUR MOTHER!"

"Edward . . ." Grammy began, but she thought better of it. "Come on, Peggy," she said gently. "Let's read a story."

Ω

When I snuck out later in the day, I found the father phoebe stiff and cold, with both his eyes pecked out. I wrapped him in a Kleenex and buried him in the orchard, murmuring a little prayer as I covered him up. The swallows took over the nest, and they were *terrible* tenants. The phoebes had sat quietly when you went in and out, but the swallows swooped into the yard if you so much as opened the door, and no matter how quietly you sat, they wouldn't feed their babies while you were there. It was, as the Great Man put it, a continual reminder of life's injustice.

Not that I needed a reminder, with Erma riding Prince by nearly every day. If life had been just, I would have had a horse, and I could have gone riding with Joan. She wasn't as keen on riding as I was, but sometimes Mr. Bartlett let her ride Tommy, his old roan work horse, and she could have shown me the trails through their maple grove, where the giant trees made the sunlight turn green, and the ground everywhere but the sledge tracks was covered with ferns. Or we could have ridden down to the lake and let the horses drink, looking out over the still water that reflected the mountains. I wondered, sometimes, where Erma rode Prince. Not those places. Joan said Erma never rode by. That was no surprise, though. There was something that kept Erma from stopping by at the neighbors. When I asked Mother what it was, she said people didn't think well of the Oldcastles. That made me feel bad about wanting to own Erma's horse, and I kept thinking I should go visit them both . . . except Avery was almost sure to be there.

In July, the fledglings left the nest, and for a few days the yard was full of swallows, swooping and diving so near the kitchen window I was afraid they'd crash into it. Somewhere in that time, I noticed Erma hadn't ridden by lately, and when I still hadn't seen her after a couple of weeks, I began to worry about Prince. Maybe Mr. Oldcastle had wickedly gambled him away. Or maybe Mr. Weller had sold him to somebody who wasn't us. Or maybe he was lame. I asked Grammy and Mother if they thought he was okay, but the way they said "Yes, of course" in the same tone—both of them—made it clear there was something I wasn't being told.

The solution was asking the Great Man, and I carefully waited until he wandered out of his study to play the piano—which, he'd explained once, was one of his ways of thinking. It was one of my favorite pieces, so I listened until he finished and said, "What's up, Snook?"

"Prince hasn't been by for a while. I'm going to the Oldcastles and see if he's okay."

"Fine," he said. "Say hello to Erma while you're there. Poor girl—she's not to blame for her family."

So he didn't know whatever it was. That meant it was one of those things Only Women Understand, which was not a good sign. But I gave him a kiss and set out, hoping he'd remember the conversation if I got in trouble later.

I hurried down the road, thinking uncomfortably about hounds and Mrs. Oldcastle and especially Avery, but when I got to the bottom of the hill, I saw Prince standing in the shade of an ancient maple tree, surrounded by black-and-white heifers. Perfect. I slid down into the almost-dry brook, crawled through the gap in the fence, and walked slowly towards him, digging a carrot out of my pocket. Everything went fine until suddenly the heifer closest to the tree heaved herself to her feet, her eyes wide and frightened. I stopped dead, but in a second all fifteen heifers had scrambled up and bolted through the thistlely grass in a panicked stampede. Prince watched them with only vague interest, so I thought I was in luck, but then a stick dropped out of the tree right onto his back, and he took off along the cow path at a snorting trot. Watching him go, I reflected sadly that at least he wasn't lame: the trot was completely square.

I turned to go, but a thud made me look back, and there was Avery, brushing bark off his bare chest. I hurried on, pretending I hadn't seen him, but he caught up with me and grabbed my arm.

"What're you doin' on our property?" he said. "I'm gonna tell my pa you were chasin' them heifers."

I yanked my arm away and walked as fast as I could to the gap in the fence. "It's not your property—it's Mr. Weller's," I said over the thumping of my heart. "And if you tell your pa, I'll tell him you threw a stick at his five hundred dollar horse."

"And *I'll* tell him it was *you* that threw it, an' he'll believe *me*, 'cause he knows what kinda family *you* come from. Commie-pinko summer snobs that take people's kids away from them."

"You're nuts! Why would my family take kids away from their parents?"

"Moral turditude. That's lawyer talk, meaning your folks can shit on us for doin' things they don't approve of." He spat into the brook. "They didn't even *ask* her."

I had jumped down into the streambed, but instead of crawling through the gap, I turned around. "You mean, someone took *Erma* away?"

"You tell me!" he sneered. "It was your folks tipped Weller off."

"Was not!" I began hotly. Then, suddenly realizing that might be what the Great Man and I didn't know, I added, "But, look, if they . . . if anybody told Mr. Weller Erma did something bad, I'll tell them all how wrong they are! Erma just *wouldn't*—"

"—Sure she would." He jumped down on top of me, reeking of sweat and smoke and manure. I squirmed away and dove for the hole, but he grabbed my legs and yanked me back over the stones. "It's time you found out. Here, lemme—"

I kicked him harder than I'd ever kicked anything, and he let go, cursing. In the second before he could pin me down, I wriggled through the hole and scrambled up on the road, almost in the path of a truck that was rattling down the hill. It slammed on its brakes, and Mr. Weller jumped out much faster than you'd think Mr. Weller could move. I wiped my face and began to explain but he brushed past me and slid down into the streambed.

"Avery!" he bellowed. "What the hell are you doin', you li'l sonofabitch!"

Avery had already run halfway across the pasture, and as I watched, still shaking, he reached the far side, climbed the wall and disappeared into the maple grove.

Mr. Weller heaved himself back onto the road, his face red and sweating. For a moment there was no sound but his heavy breathing and the sobs I was having trouble repressing. Finally, he gestured at the mud on my torn shirt and the developing bruises on my arm. "He hurt you . . . anyplace else?"

I shook my head.

"Jist scared the bejesus outta you?"

I made myself shrug. "I'm okay."

"He's real trouble," he said. "If I ketch him, I'll lick him, but you can't beat shame into a kid who don't have any." He wiped his face. "You listen to me, now. I'm gettin' rid of them Oldcastles just as fast as the law will let me. But 'til I do, you stay away from them—*all* of 'em, you hear? They're TRASH."

The word was one I was not allowed to use, but I'd heard it enough to know what it meant. "Erma's not trash!" I said. "*She* doesn't do bad things! Why get rid of *her*?!"

The way he looked at me made me realize you didn't talk to Mr. Weller like that, but after a second his face changed a little, and he said, "Your folks didn't tell you, huh? Well, *I'll* tell you: to give her a chance, that's why. Girl gits in a family way at thirteen, fourteen, an' it's all in the family, what kinda life is she gonna have? An' what am *I* gonna look like if it gits around that I tol'rate that kinda thing in a man who works fer me? 'Sbetter for everybody to send her where she's at now, safe from her pa, so she can finish school an' live decent." His eyes narrowed as they met mine. "That okay with you?"

I said "yes," because I had to, but I added, "Avery said Mother and Grammy had something to do with it. Is that true?"

"Avery don't know shit from Shinola," he said. "And like I said, you stay out of his way. I'm gonna speak to the Professor, jist to make sure he—"

"—Oh, please don't!" I begged. "I'll never come down here again, even to see Prince. I PROMISE! Cross my heart!"

He frowned. "You here 'gainst orders?"

"No, no—he told me it was okay . . . but . . ." I floundered for words. "He's . . . a classicist. He knows everything there is to know about Odysseus and Oedipus and Orestes, but he's no good at people like the Oldcastles." The mixture of incredulity, scorn, and respect that covered his grizzled face made me despair of explaining further. "Just . . . don't speak to him. Please. I promise, promise, promise . . ."

He shook his head, but it wasn't a refusal. "All right," he said, climbing stiffly into the driver's seat. "I'll be on my way. But if I ketch you down here again . . ."

The rest, if there was any, was lost as he drove off. I hurried the other way, looking uneasily from side to side in case Avery had snuck around through the woods. He hadn't, and Mother and Grammy were way out in the vegetable garden, and the Great Man was in his study, so I got myself cleaned up without having to answer any questions.

Ω

I had questions, but I knew I had to answer them myself. Listening to conversations that adults assumed went over my head had taught me that "being in a family way" was a Vermont phrase for wives who were going to have babies—but Erma wasn't a wife. She wasn't even like those wicked Radcliffe girls Mother lectured Pris about, who thought having babies would catch them husbands. But Erma didn't want to catch a husband. All she wanted to do was ride her horse. I tried to convince myself that "in a family way" could have dual meanings, like other phrases did. But nagging at the back of my mind was the look on Avery's face as he yanked me back through the fence, and the way Mr. Weller had asked me if Avery had hurt me . . . anyplace else. Every time I tried to put all the pieces together, I felt sick, so I quit. But you didn't have to see the whole picture to be scared of Avery. Or to realize something terrible had happened to Erma.

And if something terrible had happened to Erma, what was going to happen to Prince? I looked for him anxiously when we drove to the lake, which meant driving by the Oldcastles', and he was usually under his tree. Now, though, he'd gotten dusty from rolling, and his beautiful mane and tail were all stuck with burrs.

Meanwhile, it was all over town that Mr. Weller had evicted the Oldcastles, but they wouldn't leave. Every time we drove by, Mrs. Oldcastle was sitting on the porch, yelling at Avery, and Mr. Oldcastle was tinkering with the machinery in his yard as if nothing had happened. The postmaster said they were staying because they had no place else to go, and it was a shame. At the last church supper of the summer, the ladies told Grammy and Mother that Mr. Weller should get the sheriff to help him out. The guy in the gas station, who'd gone coon hunting with Oldcastle and his hounds, said Oldcastle had bragged that Weller didn't dare throw him out because he knew there'd be trouble. Joan's dad, when the Great Man asked him if that wasn't just an idle threat, allowed as how it might not be.

The last time we drove to the lake, Prince was standing in the big barn, and Mr. Weller was brushing him. The Oldcastles watched him from their porch, and you could *feel* the way they hated him just by breathing the air. I'd promised myself to shut my eyes as we went past on the way home, but a truck and trailer had blocked the road by the barn, so we had to stop. The Oldcastles were still sitting on the porch. Mr. Weller was leading Prince into the trailer.

"Ah," said the Great Man, looking at me sadly.

I swallowed hard. "Could I go say goodbye to him?"

"Better stay out of it," he began. But he stopped as Mr. Weller stepped out of the trailer and came to his window.

"Last chance," he said, with a smile that wasn't a smile. "You kin have him for a hundret bucks—that's all Joe's givin' me unless he does real well."

"Oh!" said Mother. "Is he going to a show?"

"This time of year," said Mr. Weller, "there's nothin' left but auction." He looked at me over the Great Man's shoulder. "Hey, don't cry," he said. "He's got no vices, and any kid kin ride him. That kind usually ends up in good hands." He looked back at the Great Man. "You sure, now, Professor? Can't beat the price."

"The answer's always the same," said the Great Man. "You should know that by now."

There was something in his voice that I didn't recognize, and Mr. Weller heard it.

He tipped his dirty hat, shut the trailer's back door, and waved the driver away. As the trailer disappeared around the corner, he threw a disgusted look from the baying hounds to the silent faces on the porch. He yelled something, but I couldn't hear what it was because the Great Man started the car down the hill with such a jerk that Mother grabbed the armrest and I fell back in the seat.

"The old *shyster!*" he roared. "Using a little girl's tears to make a sale!" He turned into our driveway much too fast and slammed on the brakes. None of us got out. Through my tears, I looked over the valley towards the place where the road ran up the hill to the Bartletts' farm. Pretty soon I could see the trailer driving up it.

I guess the Great Man saw it too, because he looked over his shoulder at me. "Peggy," he said in a voice that wasn't angry anymore, "we just *can't* keep a horse for you yet. It's not just the money. Neither of us knows anything about horses, and you're not old enough to take on all that by yourself. But in a few years . . ."

Mother chimed in. "You'll be taking riding lessons at home, and I've found a place for you to ride here, too. Don't cry."

But I did cry. Not because they hadn't bought Prince, either, though I knew that was what they thought. I tried to explain, but all I could choke out was "It's not *fair*, it's not *fair*!"

The Great Man cleared his throat, but before he could say anything, I jumped out of the car and ran inside to find Grammy . . . though dragging at my heels with my beach towel was the suspicion that not even Grammy could fix what had broken in my world.

Ω

When we left, with our green wood-paneled station wagon piled with suitcases, it had frosted two nights in a row, turning the early-morning grass a hoary white and the garden a mass of black, shriveled stalks. I could see my breath as I climbed into the back seat next to Grammy.

We drove out the back way, all of us looking out the windows to say goodbye until next summer. But as we got to the Oldcastles', the Great Man slowed way down.

"Good God!" he said. "Look at that!"

I was already looking—mostly at what wasn't there. No hounds. No laundry. No Mrs. Oldcastle. But most of all, no windows. From top to bottom, the house stared blindly at the barn. Inside the big barn door, Mr. Weller, Mr. Crawford, and Mr. Wolfson were stacking paneled doors and fancy woodwork against one wall.

Mr. Weller stepped out and waved. "Back to the city for the winter, eh?"

The Great Man nodded. "It looks like there has been some action here."

"Yep," said Mr. Weller. "Happen you recall that Oldcastle was supposed to fix this place up instead of payin' rent, an' didn't. Wal, the house got worse an' worse, an' there was just no keepin' the windows in those rottin' sills. So I took 'em out after the hoss left."

"But the Oldcastles were still there!" I said.

Mr. Weller shrugged. "They were there at the start, but it got a mite cold even for them. So now I'm takin' the fine old paneling and floors out of the place . . . likely it'll fall down this winter and save me a world of taxes." Mr. Wolfson shouted a question from the sagging porch. Mr. Weller nodded to all of us and walked over to look at whatever it was. As we drove on, Grammy muttered "It's God's judgment on a hard, cruel man."

I was pretty sure she meant it was God's judgment on Mr. Oldcastle, not Mr. Weller, but I might have been wrong. Because at Thanksgiving, the Oldcastles' house burned to the ground, and before the fire truck could get there, the flames set off the hay in the great white barn, and when we came back the next summer, the foundations on either side of the road were charred and bare. Folks in town agreed that Mr. Oldcastle had probably set the fire. It drifted through my mind that Avery always carried matches in his pocket, but I didn't say so. It didn't matter, anyway. The Oldcastles had disappeared.

I never did find out what happened to Prince.

Carry Me Home

The eggs wouldn't come off the pan.

They were as perfectly done as eggs got—the top of their yolks had just turned pink, so I'd pulled the pan off the burner and poured in a little cream, the way Grammy did, to make them extra special. The toast was about to pop up, the coffee had perked, and everything was ready to surprise Mother, whose footsteps I could hear coming down the stairs, through the dining room, into the kitchen . . .

"Why, Peggy! You have breakfast all ready! What a wonderful—!"

"—No it isn't. The eggs are stuck." She hesitated, and I realized I was sort of guarding the stove. I stepped to the side. "Take a look."

She lifted the lid and gave the eggs an exploratory shove with the spatula. "Did you put butter in the pan?"

"I thought butter was just for scrambled eggs."

"I see." She was trying very hard not to smile. "Well, butter in pans isn't part of a recipe. It's one of those general rules nobody talks about because it's such habit. But these look terrific. Is it all right with you if I chip them out? They'll break, which is a shame, because you've done everything else so perfectly."

I said yes, and they did break, but it wasn't a big mess because they'd overcooked while we'd been talking. Mother was kind about it, and her tired face looked happy, as opposed to fake cheerful, for the first time since Grammy had gotten sick, so I didn't feel quite as dumb as I might have.

But that morning in school, I had what Grammy would have called a revelation, like the guy in the Bible who got knocked off his horse and changed his name to my cousin Paul's. I was looking out the window at the frozen playground through the dumb Christmas decorations we'd had to make, and suddenly I was in Vermont, sitting on the warm stones in front of our house and watching the sun set. And just when the clouds flamed pink and orange against the dark evening blue, Grammy said, "You know, I think I'm going to die soon." We all stared at her. Then Mother reminded her that she'd had a physical just before we'd come to Vermont, and everything was fine. The Great Man added that looking at the sunset brought about thoughts of mortality sometimes, and you shouldn't pay attention to them. Grammy smiled her Grammy smile and that was the end of it, except I'd been really scared, not by what she'd said, but by the way she'd said it—in the tone of voice she used when she said that she'd be going downtown today, or that Pris or Liz would be coming home. As if she was looking forward to it.

That wasn't my revelation, though. What I realized, looking out that window and seeing Vermont, was that the wrongness you could feel in our house now, floating like cigarette smoke into every single room, was that Grammy *hadn't* died. She couldn't move or speak or even understand, but the hospital had saved her. The trouble was, that wasn't the way she'd wanted to be saved—in Heaven, the perfect place where it never rained in haying season or frosted before the tomatoes were ripe, and angel food cakes never fell and eggs never got stuck in pans. Instead, she was stuck in Michigan with us, alone and still in her room, where the sun never shined.

"Peggy?"

I turned around. Mrs. Morrison, my teacher, was looking at me oddly, and after I'd blinked a couple of times, I saw why. All the other kids were gone.

"Didn't you hear the bell?" she asked.

"Guess not," I said. Feeling that some sort of explanation was necessary, I added, "I was thinking about my grandmother. She had a stroke."

"Is that something you'd like to talk about?"

I looked at her concerned face, and for a moment I hesitated. Everybody said she was the best teacher at John Dewey Elementary, and she certainly was brighter than the others. But to talk to her . . .

"Hey, Jean—ready for faculty meeting?"

Mrs. Morrison swung around, and beyond her I saw Mr. Stanley. His breezy smile changed to an "oh" as she put her finger to her lips, and he backed out of the door, but I'd already made up my mind.

I smiled as well as I could. "I'm fine," I said, and to prove it I threaded my way across the room through the tables and chairs to my cubby.

Mrs. Morrison sighed. "Okay, Peggy. But any time you need somebody to talk to, remember that I care."

People had said that a lot to me lately. I realized they meant well, but it was embarrassing, so I'd cooked up a reply that stopped them. "Thank you," I said, buttoning my jacket. "I'll remember."

Ω

By the time Pris came home at the end of the week, my fried eggs came out perfectly. Mother was really proud of me, so I'd started making breakfast every day while she tended to Grammy. Sometimes she took longer than others, so I'd learned to wait on the eggs until I heard her go into the bathroom to empty the bedpan, which meant she was almost through. Of course it was different as soon as vacation started: Mother fed Grammy first, which made things start later, and the rest of us all ate together. But the Great Man and Pris were impressed by my eggs, so I kept making breakfast. I branched out into scrambled eggs, but not bacon—that was the Great Man's specialty. One day, Pris came down early and we made waffles, which we all ate with maple syrup from our very own Vermont trees, and for a little while the house smelled the way it should at Christmas time.

When we were through, Pris looked at Mother. "Did you and Daddy talk about what I said yesterday?"

Mother put her napkin in its ring. "Well, I was very . . . I mean, I'm managing perfectly well—"

"—What's this?" said the Great Man. There was a little silence while he lit his cigarette, and I could see Mother wasn't going to answer. But Pris did.

"What we were talking about was getting a private nurse," she said. "I realize a nursing home is out, but Mother can't go on this way. She's exhausted and—"

"—Yes." The Great Man took a long pull on his cigarette. "That would be a good idea, if your mother didn't feel uncomfortable about having a stranger . . ."

"But you wouldn't *have* to have a stranger!" said Pris. "Yesterday, when I took our Christmas maple syrup to the Burneys, Mrs. Burney gave me the number of the wonderful nurse they had when she broke her leg. She said you might remember her—you met her when you went to visit. Her name, would you believe, is Mrs. Love."

"Mrs. Love!" said Mother.

The Great Man laughed. "Remember her! Nobody that's seen her can forget her! She's really something! What do you think, Ellen?"

I looked from him to her. There was something they weren't saying, something that made her hesitate. I was going to ask what, but Pris jerked her head at me, and we cleared the plates, letting the kitchen door swing shut behind us. Pris set her plates into the sink a little too hard. "He should have done it *months* ago!" she muttered.

"He suggested a nurse once, but she said families should look after their own."

"Only the women," said Pris, scrubbing the maple syrup pitcher harder than it deserved. "'Self-sacrifice is a woman's crowning glory.' Or so we're taught."

Pris and her—that is, our—older, married sister Liz often talked about Mother as if they knew more than she did. Defending her only made them go on longer, so I didn't try. "It's neat that Mrs. Burney suggested somebody they know," I said. "Is her name really Mrs. Love?"

"If it isn't, it's the name she goes by," snapped Pris. "And I hope to God she comes. Mother's just at the end of her rope. *Nobody* can be a full-time nurse to her mother, especially . . . " She gave me an odd look. "Grammy's been in our family all your life, hasn't she?"

"Sure."

"Funny," she said. "Your childhood's so different from Liz's and mine. No Grammy for us until we were older than you are now." I stared at her, trying to imagine it, and suddenly she smiled. "We always said you were a present to Grammy. She just *loved* having you around." She patted my head. "Now, though, it's really tough on Mother; she can't go *anywhere*, and she's doing awful, heavy, dirty work instead of writing and politicking—and hey, listen, can you try a little harder, Peggy? She's got enough to worry about without coping with you."

"What've I been doing?"

"Nothing most spoiled nine-year-olds don't do, I suppose,"

she said. "Back-talking, being messy, going into a rage when you don't get your way . . ."

I'd begun to tune her out, but this stopped me, because I'd thought I'd kept those rages a secret. Maybe Mother had figured them out when I'd asked for a punching bag for Christmas. Or maybe it was the pillows I'd beaten the stuffing out of. Or the paper dolls I'd ripped apart. Or . . . but Pris had stopped.

I looked up sulkily. "I'm not *all* bad. I make breakfast every morning."

"Of course you're not all bad," she said impatiently. Suddenly she cocked her head. "Hey, I think he's on the phone!" She put her finger to her lips, so we tiptoed towards the dining room and peeked around the door. Sure enough, he was on the hall phone, and mother was hovering on the bottom step of the staircase. "Yes," he said. "Yes. Fine." Then he smiled. "Wonderful. We'll see you at eight tomorrow morning."

He hung up, walked to the staircase, and gave Mother a kiss. "She said the case she'd been working on had just finished and she was looking for another. It couldn't be better."

I couldn't hear Mother's answer, because Pris was doing a victory dance all around the table.

Ω

At exactly eight o'clock, the doorbell rang. The Great Man and Pris weren't up yet, and Mother was tending to Grammy, so I opened the door—and saw what Mother and the Great Man hadn't said. The woman who swept in, ensconced in a red coat with a fur collar, was black—but very different from the black people who came to our house at the back door. Somehow her presence paralyzed me, and I stood like an idiot, wondering if she was maybe a queen in disguise, while she set down her patent leather purse, removed her hat, gloves, and finally the coat, and stood before me, immaculate in a starched white uniform with a little pin that said Amelia Love, RN.

"I'm Mrs. Love," she said, holding out her free hand. "I'm here for your Granny." As my hand disappeared in hers, she looked around the hall. "Where shall I put my things?"

"In the closet," I whispered. Then, as my manners came back in a belated rush, "I'll take them." She handed me the coat, and I took the opportunity to stroke its soft collar. "That's really nice."

"Why, thank you," she said.

I found a hanger and cleared a spot for her coat between ours, put her hat and gloves on the side table, and pointed to the staircase. "Grammy's upstairs," I said. "I'll show you."

When we got to Grammy's sunless room, Mother looked up, her face a mixture of defensiveness and relief. "I'm Ellen Hamilton," she said. "We're very grateful to you. My mother had a stroke in October, and—"

"—I've read the case," said Mrs. Love. And to our surprise, she leaned over Grammy and held out her hand. "Hello, Mrs. Gottenheben. I'm Amelia Love, and I'll be taking care of you today."

"Oh, she can't underst—" Mother started. But she stopped, because although Grammy's hand didn't move at all, her eyes rested on Mrs. Love's face.

Mrs. Love looked back at Grammy attentively. "Your little granddaughter has very nice manners," she said. "She's right here—Step this way, honey—Can you see her?"

I stepped the way she said to, looked at Grammy—and met her eyes. "Hi, Grammy," I said, hardly daring to hope that the recognition in her face was real.

"It's . . . it's a miracle," said Mother.

"Not at all," said Mrs. Love. "The records say it's mostly a left-hemisphere stroke, though there seems to be some damage on the right, too. That means she can't talk, but it's possible for her to understand what's said to her. I'd say she could understand everything that happens in this room, if she chose to. So our job is to get her to choose." She turned towards Grammy's tray, where a soft boiled egg and toast were waiting. "That hers? I'll give it to her while you go eat your own."

It was more or less an order, but we couldn't take it right away, because the Great Man and Pris appeared in the door, and Mrs. Love shook hands with them in a businesslike manner before sitting down in what had been Mother's chair next to Grammy. Then we all went downstairs, and I made four perfect fried eggs, and Pris insisted on taking Mother out shopping, and the Great Man said reflectively that the word for Mrs. Love was *magnificent*.

When everybody left, I went up to Grammy's room, feeling bad because I hadn't gone there more often. I'd hoped to see if Grammy would know who I was again, but she was asleep. Mrs. Love was sitting near the window, reading.

"Would you like a cup of coffee?" I said.

"Why, that would be very nice, honey," she said. "Cream and sugar."

I went downstairs and got it, being careful not to spill any in the saucer. She took it with a smile and put her book down. "My, that's nice and hot. You make it?"

I nodded, but I was looking at her book, which opened flat, the way a book did when you read it a lot. On one page there was a stylized picture of terrified horses and men with spears, overpowered by curled waves. And on the page opposite, yellow lettering said "Let My People Go." "Oh!" I said. "Is the picture Moses and the Red Sea?"

"It sure is, honey. See Moses and his people, there, getting away?"

I hadn't, but now that I looked, I did. "It's a wonderful picture," I said. "It really understands how scared those horses are."

Mrs. Love smiled. "It's a wonderful book," she said, shutting it to show me the title.

"*God's Trombones*," I read. "So it's music?"

"No. It's old-time sermons, only in poetry."

"But 'Let my people go' is part of a song."

Instead of answering, she smiled and sang softly, *When Israel was in Egypt's land, Let my people go; Oppress'd so hard they could not stand, Let my people go.*

She seemed to expect me to join in on the chorus, so I did, though I felt a little funny about it.

"You have a sweet voice," she said, handing me back the cup. "And it's a fine old song. Now, you let me read a while, and when your granny wakes up, I'll let you know so you can visit."

I took the cup back to the kitchen, the song drifting around me. It had drifted around the Great Man, too, because by the time I'd washed the cup, he was sitting at the piano, playing it with the interesting harmonies that always seemed to spring from his fingers. From there he went to "Swing Low, Sweet Chariot," all moody and sad. I leaned against the living room door and listened until he went upstairs to work on the idea that had come to him while he played. Then I sat down on the still warm bench and sounded out "Swing Low, Sweet Chariot"—which seemed more . . . well, okay . . . for a person like me to play, though there was no denying that "Go Down, Moses" was a terrific song.. After I'd played for a while, an idea about Grammy came to me, but I wasn't quite sure what to do with it.

Ω

I kept on being not quite sure for a long time, and the reason was Mrs. Love. She seemed to know what Grammy wanted by just looking at her, and after she pointed out that Grammy often listened to us, Mother started reading to me in Grammy's room, and when we read *A Little Princess*, Grammy looked positively furious at the way Miss Minchin treated Sara. Mrs. Love said that was wonderful; it meant Grammy was getting better, and the more we talked to her, the better she'd get. So until school started again, I visited her five or six times a day, which should have given me a chance to ask the question that was bothering me, but the other side of Mrs. Love kept stopping me.

The other side was what happened one evening after Pris had gone back to Radcliffe, when Mrs. Love had stayed late because Mother and the Great Man were going out to dinner for the first time since Halloween. I was supposed to take a bath, and I did, and then I curled up in bed with *The Good Master* and was reading away when Mrs. Love appeared in the door.

"You're not finished with your bath."

If I hadn't been so involved in the book, I would have noticed there was no "honey" at the end of her sentence, but I didn't. "Sure I am," I said. "See? I'm all clean."

"The bathroom's a *mess*."

"Oh, that," I said, shrugging. "Mother'll pick it up when she comes home."

Mrs. Love took two steps forward. "You get in that bathroom and clean it up *yourself!*" she said. "You got no *right* to make your mother wait on you!"

Her face rocketed me out of bed and sent me fleeing down the hall, but as I picked up my things—towel, washcloth, underpants, slip, blouse, skirt, sweater, shoes, socks, hairbrush, hairdryer, toothbrush, toothpaste—I was distracted by the novelty of her words. I was inured to sisterly litany of my offenses, but this scolding (I recognized it from books, though I couldn't remember having had one before) somehow presented me to myself in a new light. There was no time to reflect; Mrs. Love's approaching steps made me look anxiously at the fleet of wooden boats clustered around the drain. Surely, picking up couldn't include . . . my new insight, unfinished though it was, immediately included them. I hurriedly stacked my folded clothes on the stool, and as Mrs. Love opened the door, I was putting the last boat in dry dock under the sink.

Mrs. Love looked in, looked around, looked at me, and left without a word. An hour later, she said "Goodnight, honey," in a perfectly friendly voice when I tiptoed in to give Grammy a kiss. But for weeks afterwards, I could feel her presence at my elbow, informing me that I had no *right* to leave my coat on the hall sofa, no *right* to leave my shoes in the living room, no *right* to leave my bed for Mother to make, or—the list seemed endless, but I was willing to do anything it took to avoid the scorn I'd seen in her face. Including not asking her the question that had come to me at the piano.

The question kept bugging me, especially because after a couple of months of getting so much better that she could almost smile when I came into her room, Grammy froze. There was a hubbub about it; Mrs. Love told Mother, who called the doctor, who came and shook his head and said we'd just have to see. So we were very patient, but she ate less and less, and I wasn't sure she knew who I was any more. I still came in from school to say hi to her, though, and one day, Mrs. Love was reading a black book with pages in two columns. Grammy was asleep, so I asked "Is that the Bible?"

"Sure is," she said, smiling. "I thought maybe you'd like to hear the story behind that song you sing all the time."

"Which song?" I asked.

"You'll know the second you hear this." Her voice deepened: "And it came to pass, as they—that's the prophet Elijah and his friend Elisha, honey—still went on, and talked, that, behold, there appeared a chariot of fire, and horses of fire, and parted them both asunder; and Elijah went up by a whirlwind into heaven."

"Oh!" I said, delighted. "'Swing Low, Sweet Chariot!'"

She nodded. "Must've been a grand sight, seeing the old man swept to heaven like that."

"I'll say! I wish—" I broke off as I glanced at Grammy, all still in the bed, but Mrs. Love's face showed me she knew what I'd been wishing. She didn't seem shocked or angry, though, so the question I'd been not asking all that time came tumbling out. "Is thinking that Grammy wants to go to heaven—not in a chariot or anything, just the usual way, instead of lying here—is that the same as wanting her to die?"

"Oh, no, honey. *Everybody* wants folks they love to go straight to heaven with as little pain as can be."

"So it's not wicked?"

"What's a little girl like you got to do with wicked?"

"I just wanted to be sure."

"You can be sure," she said, a little shortly. "Youngsters living how and where you do got no call to be wicked." I must have looked puzzled, because her eyes softened, and she added, "Nobody can see you with your granny and think you want anything for her but an easier passage to the other side."

I looked at the still face on the pillow, and the fear that had been nagging at me in the past couple of weeks crystallized into an awareness of what had made me afraid. I looked back at Mrs. Love and realized that she'd been watching me. "Um," I said, "Does that mean she's not going to get better?"

"That's what it means," she said. "Some strokes, a person can get better from. But strokes that affect the brain stem, like the one she had a few weeks ago—well, she didn't get better right away, so she's not going to." She paused, maybe waiting for me to cry, but I didn't, so she went on. "And so now we got to switch from the kind of nursing that helps her get well to the kind that carries her Home."

Home. I looked at Grammy's still, waiting face, and suddenly I saw a band of angels throw open the sunless window so a great chariot could sweep in. The beautiful, fiery horses snorted in excitement as Someone swept Grammy up, bedclothes and all, and carried her out of Michigan, across Canada and New York to Vermont, where He gently set her down. As she stood (stood!), looking at Joan's mowing against the backdrop of Haystack Mountain, the angels clothed her all in white, and she walked (walked!) along the garden, admiring the crocuses, daffodils, and violets. Then the angels gave her a steadying arm across the ditch, and she wandered out into the orchard, and there among the pink and white blossoms, Grandfather, who'd died just before I was born, held out both hands to her, and Mother's brother who had died in college kissed her on both cheeks, and her little baby who had died just after he'd learned to walk toddled through the grass to be swept up in her arms, and they all looked at the mountains in their delicate green, and they said, yes, this was Home, this was Heaven, this was where everybody wanted to be.

"Honey, you okay?"

The vision faded back into Grammy, still and sleeping. "Does Mother know?"

"Sure she does. So does your father."

"They haven't said anything about it."

"Sometimes saying things makes them seem too certain."

I looked out the window that my chariot had plunged through a few minutes ago. The big elm tree just outside it was beginning to bud. I'd only worn a sweater when I walked to school today. "My father says Heaven is just a story," I said bleakly.

Mrs. Love shook her head. "That's what he *says*, like plenty other smart men. But the way he plays those fine old songs on the piano shows how deep the story's fixed in his soul."

"Then it's . . . a real story? Like Napoleon or George Washington?"

"Honey," she said, drawing me to her, "life here on this earth is so confused and uncertain, half the time you can't tell what's real from what's not real. But Napoleon and George Washington and the rest of them—and the rest of us—we're all part of the Great Story, and at the end, across the river, the Almighty takes care of us." For a moment we stayed very still, watching Grammy together. Then she looked at her watch and stood up. "Time for me to get your granny some of that good chicken broth your mama makes. Did you put the cookies away after you took one?"

I zipped down the back stairs and had the jar where it belonged before she got there.

Ω

About a week later, as the eggs and I were waiting impatiently for the bedpan-emptying stage, Mother called down the back stairs that there were extra things to do, and could I get myself off to school without her coming down? Something was obviously up, but it was already 7:35 and I usually left at 7:30, so I took off, munching on a piece of toast with peanut butter and imagining what Grammy would say if she knew I was eating in the street as if I hadn't any family. I wondered, on and off, why Mother's voice had sounded so different, but the day was filled with long division that I got mostly wrong and a spelling test that I got mostly right, and an election in which I was voted class treasurer, which surprised me, because even though positions like that didn't mean much, only popular kids got them. I knew Mother would be pleased, so when I opened the back gate and found her in the garden, I jiggled the treasurer's box.

"Look!" I said. "I'm a class officer!"

She looked—she even said that was wonderful—but I could tell by the way she put down her trowel that she was thinking of something else. "Peggy," she said slowly. "Peggy . . . your little Grammy died today."

I started to object that Grammy wasn't little, just shorter than everybody else in the family except me, but suddenly the rest of what she'd said hit me, and I stood very still, the treasurer's box in my hands, staring unbelievingly at the lilacs and the forsythia and the tulips and the perfect sunshine. Gradually, the purple and yellow and red swam together as tears poured silently out of my eyes. I'd never cried that way before.

Mother stepped quickly out of the garden and put her arms around me, but that squished the treasurer's box against me and I pulled away. "What . . . what happened?"

"Mrs. Love said she had a second brain stem stroke." Mother's voice, which had been shaky, changed to just barely normal. "A blessing, she called it—Grammy's face was so peaceful, you could see she'd been taken without any pain."

I looked up at the brilliant blue sky, then at Mother. "Taken . . . across the River? So she's in Heaven now, all well?"

"Across the River," she said, almost smiling. "Where did you pick that up?"

"From the song," I said impatiently. "*'I looked over Jordan, and what did I see.'* The Jordan's the river you have to cross to get to Heaven. And that's where she is, now, right? It's not just a story?"

"Of course Grammy has gone to Heaven, dear," said Mother, in the same tone of voice she used to tell me there were no ghosts under the bed or lions in the closet. She gave me another quick hug and added, "Shirley and her mother are going to come pick you up in a few minutes. I put some things into a bag for you, but you'd better go be sure they're what you want."

Except for Joan in Vermont, Shirley was my best friend, and her grandmother had died a year or so ago, so she'd know how I felt. But . . . "I'm going to spend a *school* night at Shirley's?"

"Daddy and I are going to be very busy here," she said. "There are lots of things to be organized, and it won't be very cheerful."

I would much rather have stayed at home being un-cheerful with them, but Mrs. Love's voice whispered in my ear that I had *no right* to argue with Mother when she was so tired and upset, so I went inside, climbed the stairs, and put the treasurer's box in the back of my closet. After I made some corrections to the bag Mother had packed for me, I must have stopped thinking about what I was doing, because my feet walked me around the corner and down the narrow hall that led to Grammy's room.

The Great Man was leaning against her doorway, looking in. "She's not here," he said, turning around.

"Yeah, I know. Mother told me." I stopped a few feet short of him. "Can I look?"

"Sure you want to?"

"You mean, I shouldn't even . . . ?"

"No, no, go ahead," he said. "Just brace yourself."

I slipped by him—and stood transfixed. Grammy's bed was stripped, right down to the mattress; the bed pad and her blankets were folded in perfect squares next to the blue-and-white striped uncovered pillows. The bedspread she'd crocheted was gone. So were her medicines, her glasses, the chair that had been Mother's and Mrs. Love's. Her jewelry box, her silver-backed hairbrush set, and her collection of family pictures had been cleared off the top of her dresser. The warm breeze blowing in the window my chariot had flown through mixed with a faint smell of Spic and Span.

The Great Man's hand fell on my shoulder, a slender column of smoke rising from his cigarette. "Mrs. Love was wonderful," he said. "Called the funeral home, stayed here until they took the cor—er, your grandmother away, helped Mother clean the room. Efficient, kind, sympathetic. What a professional."

"I was sort of hoping she'd still be here," I said, looking around forlornly.

He gave my shoulder a pat. "They finished a couple of hours ago. There was no reason for her to stay. Actually, there was probably no reason for her even to come, but Mother needed someone to confirm—"

"—Wait! Mrs. Love wasn't here when Grammy had the stroke?"

"No, it seems the stroke happened a bit after midnight and Grammy died instantly, in her sleep." He looked out the window. "It's a good way to go."

"A good way to go!" My voice broke. "Alone? In the dark? Without Mrs. Love and me to help her get Home?"

The eyes behind his dusty glasses suddenly looked interested. "Was that how you'd scripted it?"

"Scripted it?"

"Told yourself a story about how it was going to happen. Usually influenced by Victorian novels." He smiled sympathetically. "There's no harm in it, if that's what's bothering you. The trouble is, we can't make people's stories turn out the way we want. If we could, Grammy would never have lingered on like this." He raised his hand off my shoulder and took a puff of his cigarette. "I always liked her, you know. And she was wonderful with you."

I nodded, hoping he'd say something like she was okay now, but the doorbell rang, so I hurried downstairs to let Shirley and her mother in. As I got into their car, I looked up at the window in Grammy's room, and then down at the big, open living room window below it. The Great Man was sitting at the piano, but I couldn't hear what he was playing.

Ω

Scripting. So it wasn't just something I did: it had a name. The idea got more and more puzzling, because it seemed that people's lives got scripted as well as their deaths, depending on who was telling the story. When my uncles and aunts came for the funeral, Mother got out all the pictures of Grammy, and everybody talked about them, and it didn't take much watching and listening to realize that there was a character called "Mother" in their stories who was very different from the Grammy who was an extra in our family, like me. "Mother" had four sisters and a rich brother who had sent all her children to college; "Mother" had worshipped "Dad" for his gentleness, and she'd run a wonderful household of kids who played in the barn and went roller skating. Most important, "Mother" lived in Ohio, which was so much Home to her that her body was going to be shipped there and buried in the family plot. When I suggested that the apple orchard in Vermont would be a better place to bury Grammy than a cemetery nobody lived near enough to visit, there was a silence while everybody looked at everybody else, and I realized that the "Mother" in my uncles' stories had never watched a Vermont sunset or picked early Vermont apples and made them into pies.

Mrs. Love had been right: life was so confusing and uncertain, it was hard to tell what was real from what wasn't. Since children didn't go to funerals or burials, the grownups' story was the "real" that made things happen, and there was no need to tell me I had no *right* to be any trouble while everybody was busy and sad. So I was very good—everybody said so—except for once, and nobody knew about that because I hid the evidence. The punching bag I'd gotten for Christmas was the kind on a flexible stick that screwed into a platform you stood on while you hit it. When the Great Man put it together the first time, he shook his head and said the set-up would never survive a real punch. It didn't; time after time, I'd sent the bag and stick flying across the basement. But when it went flying this time, the shoddiness of the whole contraption so infuriated me that I picked up the stupid bag by the stick and beat it against the laundry table. By the time the bag finally split, I was shaking so hard that I sat down for a long time, terrified by what I'd done and how angry I'd been as I did it.

Ω

Somewhere in the back of my mind, I'd treasured the hope of finding the *real* Grammy—or at least the Grammy of my stories—in Vermont. When we finally got there, I ran up the stairs through the waiting house and stood in her room, hoping her stuff would tell me she was still somehow around . . . but though there was the same old wallpaper and the same old pictures, the room was almost bare. Plain white bedspread. Plain white bureau with nothing in it or on it—not even hair pins. I opened the closet hopefully. No house dresses. No old fashioned shoes. No hand-knit sweaters. Nothing but a surprised mouse that scuttled into its hole. For a moment I stood stock still, trying to think how it was possible . . . then I remembered that Pris had volunteered to drive up from Radcliffe and empty Grammy's room, and Mother had said that would be wonderful.

I walked slowly to my own room and pulled my stuffed animals out of their chest so the mothball smell would fade. I was about to go through my drawers to look for some Vermont clothes when I saw a picture on the dresser top. A picture of Grammy. Unlike the pictures Mother and my uncles had been talking about, this one was in color—a snapshot the Great Man had taken of her last summer. It was her seventy-fifth birthday, and she was all dressed up to go out to lunch with Mother and me. She was standing in a shaft of sunlight, looking out the back door—probably waiting for Mother to bring the car, but if you didn't know that, her expression would make you think she was waiting patiently for the chariot. I picked it up, looking first at Grammy's wonderfully familiar face, then at the pretty inlaid frame that decorated it.

Behind me, Mother's footsteps struggled up the steep stairs, bumping something heavy. "Peggy? Here's your suitcase. Can you unpack—?" She stopped, looking at the picture. "What's that?"

I showed it to her wordlessly.

She looked at it for a long time, and when she smiled at me, there were tears in her eyes. "You have a really nice sister, Peggy."

"I what?"

"I had a print made of the slide, and I sent it to Pris last fall. She must have had it framed and left it for you when she . . . she emptied . . ." Mother gave me a hug. "Anyway, it was nice of her." She looked at the peaceful, waiting face that shone between my hands. "I'd forgotten what a wonderful picture it is," she said softly. "It's like having her back."

I nodded. "Yeah. It really is."

Red Letter Days

The summer after Grammy died, we stayed with Mr. Zander for ten days in July because Mother and the Great Man were painting the floors in our house. When I offered to help, they said Mr. Zander wanted my company. I was a little concerned—Mr. Zander's desire for my company expired quickly unless I maintained flawlessly adult behavior—but I tried hard, and it was worth it. Long ago, after I'd asked him why the woman who'd spent the summer with him wasn't Mrs. Zander, he'd explained that when you lived with somebody and kept your eyes open, you got to know what they were really like. He was right. During those ten days, I found out all sorts of things about Mr. Zander that you wouldn't notice if you just knew him from parties at his house or ours.

One of the things I realized was how interesting his house was. He had inherited it from his mother, who had inherited it from her father, who had come over from Sweden to farm in Vermont, bringing with him an enormous hand-carved wooden mantelpiece that he'd installed in the living room. It would have looked better in a room five times the size, but Mr. Zander said that when you lived in your grandfather's house you had to live with history, and so he'd left it there. Living with history also meant living with bookshelves that were stuffed with books in Swedish and Norwegian and Russian and French and German, along with the complete Sherlock Holmes, the Hardy Boys, and other things Mr. Zander had read as a kid when he'd spent summers visiting his grandfather.

Another thing I learned was that the farm had been Mr. Zander's only solid home, because his father had been a newspaper reporter who had traveled all over Europe and even to Russia, taking his wife and kid with him. All that traveling made Mr. Zander different from most people we knew, even though he'd gone to Yale and was a professor like the other men. He spoke all the languages in his books, and he was what the Great Man called a European intellectual, which I gradually figured out meant you really had to respect him, but you couldn't quite trust his ideas.

Most of those ideas were political—not like Mother's politics, which had to do with the Democrats and getting out the vote, but more about equality and justice. The second day I was staying with him, we were thinning carrots, and he asked, "Does it bother you that we're being unfair?"

"Unfair?"

"Sure. Are the carrots we're pulling up any less deserving than the ones we're not pulling up?"

I frowned. "Mother says you're supposed to pull out the small ones so the big ones will do better."

"The standard capitalist attitude," he said. "Encourage the great, uproot the small."

I looked at the baby carrots in my hand, suddenly horrified.

"Hey, it's okay!" he said. "It's just that when you start thinking about gardening, you realize . . . well, look at those weeds marching into the squash plants. They're imperialists, right? You have to defend your territory all the time."

I looked at them, considering. "I suppose they think they have a perfect right to be there."

"Exactly!" he said. "I've got great hopes for you, Peggy."

I wasn't sure what he was hoping for, but I took the little carrots inside and carefully ate them so they wouldn't be wasted.

A few days later, Mr. Zander and I were whizzing up a hill in his MG, singing "Polly-wolly-doodle-all-the-day"—and suddenly a jeep shot over the top and flew towards us with all its wheels off the ground. The MG went crazy, swerving and skidding to a stop so fast that I had to grab the edge of the windshield to keep myself from flying out. As I clung there, the jeep flashed past in a teetering red blur and landed with its right-hand wheels so far up the bank that its driver had to roll out to keep it from tipping over. In sudden stillness, I loosened my grip and turned shakily to Mr. Zander.

He wasn't there.

For a second, I thought the Jeep had hit him, but his door was open, and he was standing in the road next to the other driver.

"Who the hell do you think you are?" he said in a voice that made me shiver.

As the guy looked up, I recognized him—Jack Weller. He lived in Westover with his mother because Mr. Weller had walked out on them, but he strutted around at our baseball evenings with guys like himself or girls who thought tough was cool. Mr. Bartlett always gave Rob, Joan, and me strict instructions to stay out of his way, because he was trouble. Like now. He jumped up with his fists ready for action.

Mr. Zander dropped his hands to his sides. "Come off it, Jack," he said. "I'm not going to hit you. But how about an apology? Your idiocy damn near killed a little girl."

Jack glanced my way, and when our eyes met, his face changed from surly to something nastier. "Little girl, huh?" he said over his shoulder. "Sure. Jest like th' one in the book by that Red—"

Mr. Zander spun him around and held him under his chin by the collar of his T-shirt. I watched, mesmerized, as Jack tried to wrestle himself free, calling him a mothersomething Commie, but Mr. Zander just held him there, not saying anything—then heaved him backwards on the bank next to his Jeep and stood over him. For a long time, they stared at each other; then Jack muttered something I couldn't hear. Mr. Zander nodded, strode to the MG, and spun out in a great rush of gravel.

Neither of us said anything until we got back to his house, and when he turned off the engine, we both sat still, watching the sun flickering through the trees. After a while I said, "That was scary."

"It sure was," he said. "I'm really sorry. The idiot was jumping the bump—it's a great sport on this road, but sensible kids post a friend at the top."

"I don't think Jack has many friends."

"Comes as no surprise," he said grimly.

"You gonna have him arrested?"

"No. I'd love to see him lose his license . . . but, well, I was a kid once myself."

"Wild? Like him?"

"Not just like him. Less nasty. Different politics. But with cars, wild enough."

I looked at him, trying to imagine his face younger, his eyes resentful, his open-at-the throat blue work shirts and square shoulders replaced by T-shirts and a slouch. I couldn't, but the effort reminded me of the question I'd meant to ask.

"What did he mean about my being like a girl in that book by a Red?"

"There's a book a lot of people are talking about these days," said Mr. Zander. "The main character's a girl about your age, but she's nothing like you. She came to Jack's mind as part of a blanket insult. You can tell, because what really damned the book in his eyes was its being written by a Red. Ridiculous—Nabokov isn't a Red. Just a Russian."

"What *is* a Red, if it's not a Russian?"

His eyebrows rose. "You don't know?"

"Is it like a Communist?"

"There you go. Sure."

"Wait a sec," I said, thinking fast. "McCarthy was censored, right?

"Censured. There's a difference."

"Censured, then—but doesn't that mean calling somebody a Commie or a Red is . . . out of date?"

"Not everywhere. As you heard. I bet you'll hear some of it even in your sheltered circles."

"Mother's *against* McCarthy! And even the Great Man got mad about his lists!"

He nodded. "Sure. And they're members of the ADA. Good liberals."

I looked at him indignantly. "You make it sound as if liberals aren't the good guys!"

"Oh, they are—just not good *enough* guys. My uncles and cousins in the Old Country pay taxes so everybody gets free schooling and free doctors, and nobody gets more of anything until everybody has enough. If we had that over here, everybody'd be better off."

"Free doctors! That's socialized medicine!"

"It sure is, and the sooner we get it, the better."

I stared at him. "But . . . but socialized medicine is un-American!"

"Good God, Peggy! Where did you pick *that* up?"

"At school."

"From your teachers?"

"Uh-uh. But the kids know."

"All of them?"

You had to be very careful when you disagreed with Mr. Zander, because he argued by the Socratic method, which meant he kept asking questions until you said something stupid. So I thought a minute. "Not all. Mostly the ones whose fathers are doctors. But they're the ones who would know."

"No, they'd be the ones whose fathers think socialized medicine would make them lose money. And if you think something is going to make you lose what you have, current propaganda makes it easy to say it's un-American."

"But you're not supposed to *believe* propaganda! You're supposed to think!"

"I rest my case," he said, smiling.

"No, wait! If you think socialized stuff is okay, doesn't that make you a Red?"

He laughed and got out of the car. "Let's compromise on Pink," he said. "Like we're both going to be if we sit here in the sun instead of having lunch."

Ω

That afternoon, Mother had scheduled me to play with Joan, but when we got to the Bartletts' farm, everybody except Rex, their collie dog mix, was working in the mowing, and the sky looked so threatening that Mr. Zander wrestled up the top on the MG and said we'd better get out there to help. So we got out there, and it was as wonderful as haying always was, with the smell of dried grass, the bales plopping out of the baler, which Rob was old enough to drive now, and Mr. Bartlett throwing the bales up on the truck as if they weighed nothing at all. This time it was exciting, too, because we could see black clouds rolling across the mountains, filled with thunder and lightning. Mr. Zander was a *real* help, standing on the bouncing truck and stacking bales as fast as Mr. Bartlett tossed them up. Joan and I rolled the bales towards them, feeling the wind get cooler and wetter as the sky over us went dark.

Drops started to fall just as Mrs. Bartlett got the truck to the barn, but Mr. Bartlett and Mr. Zander tossed the bales through the loft door to Rob before they even got damp. Joan and I had scurried up to the loft, and we had just finished moving a litter of kittens out of the way when the clouds opened up with crashes and flashes and huge drops. After everything was stacked, we all sat around the loft door watching the trees toss in the wind, the backs of their leaves showing white against the black sky.

I loved watching storms, and I was about to lean out—but suddenly something snapped and banged at almost the same time. I jumped back, and as I landed, the whole barn shook. Mr. Bartlett grinned. "Best stay inside," he said, pushing the door shut.

I quickly sat next to Mr. Zander. He started to put an arm around me, then stopped and asked if I was all right. I remembered adult behavior and said I was, which made me feel very brave, since Joan had hidden her face in Mrs. Bartlett's shoulder, and Rob's eyes got bigger and bigger as one snap and bang followed another. After six or seven snaps and crashes, Mr. Zander looked at Mr. Bartlett. "Pretty impressive lightning rods you have."

"Good thing," said Mr. Bartlett. "I ain't been through this kinda fire since '45."

"Oh yeah?" said Mr. Zander. "What division were you in?"

"Fifth infantry." He said it in his usual voice, but if he'd said he'd written five books, Mr. Zander couldn't have looked more impressed.

"My God!" he said. "The Red Diamonds?"

"The Red Devils, is more like it!" said Rob proudly. "Those guys won the Battle of the Bulge an' rescued Chartres, an' took Frankfurt from the Huns an'—"

"Rob," interposed Mr. Bartlett mildly. "You know I don't like them sorts of words." He looked at Mr. Zander in a new sort of way. "You were over there?"

"Oh yeah," said Mr. Zander. "But the closest I came to action was boot camp. The Brass found out I could translate, so I spent my two years sitting at a desk."

"Where?"

Mr. Zander shrugged. "Frankfurt, Berlin—"

"—That's where Dad got his medals!" said Joan. "Both of 'em!"

Mr. Bartlett waved her words away and opened the loft door a little. It was still raining, but the thunder had rolled on and the lightning was just flashing idly. "Nothin' a medal could do fer that terrible mess at the end," he said, looking out. "All those folks with no place to go, farms and little towns shot to hell . . ."

Mr. Zander nodded without saying anything, and as I looked from him to Mr. Bartlett in the hay-smelling silence, I suddenly realized that The War was a lot more than a story that grownups mentioned in passing.

Mr. Bartlett turned back to the loft. "Y'know," he said, "when I signed up, I thought maybe I'd git some more education after discharge an' try my hand at a desk job. But by the end, seeing all them places, I jist wanted to come home an' farm."

Exactly. What sane person would do anything else? I smiled at him and joined Joan, who had climbed over some bales to be sure the kittens hadn't been frightened by the storm. They were fine, tumbling around clumsily as if nothing had happened. I picked up the all-gray one I particularly liked, feeling it purr as it settled in my arms. Behind us, the grownups somehow switched from the Red Army to the Red Scare, and both Bartletts said that Red Scare talk was a terrible example to youngsters—not that you should trust the Russians too far, Mr. Bartlett added. They sure took over Europe fast enough—you had to watch 'em all the time.

I climbed back over the bales and grinned at Mr. Zander, thinking of the weeds in his garden. That accidentally ended the talking, because seeing me reminded Mrs. Bartlett that it was time for us to go get the cows in. So out we trooped into the long sunlight that had followed the storm, and Rob untied Rex, who jumped all over us, moaning in a collie voice about how awful it had been under the barn all by himself in that terrible thunder, but at a word from Mr. Bartlett, he sobered up and trotted off. We followed him, because he always knew exactly where the cows were—which, this time, was at the bottom of the pasture. My sneakers were sopped by the time we even got to the gate, and pushing through the hardhack and ferns that the cows hadn't eaten left me wet to the knees, but I didn't care. Mist was rising wispily off the lake, and the half-visible mountains behind it were a secretive blue. The air smelled of wet fern, then of cows when we got to them. We spread out and walked behind them up the hill, listening to the cowbells that clunked around the leaders' necks. It was as close to heaven as you could get without actually visiting Grammy. But after I gave her a secret invisible kiss, I found myself thinking of how it would all look if it were in a war and the Red Army was marching along, taking everything, burning down the house and barns . . . I shuddered.

"What's the matter?" asked Joan.

"Nothing," I said. Then I remembered that Joan and Rob didn't go to John Dewey Elementary, which meant that they studied useful things I didn't. So I added, "I was thinking about war and the Reds. What do they want, anyway?"

"Oh gee," said Joan. "We had a test on it last May . . . lemme think."

Rob gave her a boy-are-you-dumb look. "If it's the one they gave us, you were supposed to check the boxes that said something about a conspiracy by guys who work in factories. Dad says it's all foolishness, though. An' really, the only thing you gotta pay attention to is the bomb. They could drop it on us, and poof—we'd be like the Japs."

"*My* Dad says *that's* all foolishness," I said, not as confidently as I would have if it had indeed been the Great Man who'd said it, not Mother.

"I dunno," said Joan, "On TV, they say——" She stopped, because the cows had reached to top of the hill, and we swung the gate open so Rex could herd them down the muddy track that led to the two barns. When we got there, my parents were talking to Mrs. Bartlett and Mr. Zander in the dooryard, so I never found out what they said on TV.

But I did find out what they said on short wave radio. Sort of, anyway. Mr. Zander had one, and the Great Man was fascinated by it, so after supper all three grownups went into his study and listened to broadcasts in languages I couldn't understand, mixed with a lot of static. I wandered in and found Sherlock Holmes under D for Doyle next to a set of volumes whose names I couldn't read but Mr. Zander had told me were by a Russian named Dostoyevsky. I listened to the strange language for a second and asked what it was all about. Mother said briefly, "the Russians and the arms race," and turned back to the radio.

It wasn't dark yet, so I took Sherlock Holmes out onto the porch, which overlooked the big mountain that was beginning to have ski trails cut in it. I'd read two whole stories before Mr. Zander turned off the radio and the three of them talked over the possibility of a third world war. It wouldn't be like the last one, they agreed. Over in a couple of hours, said Mr. Zander. We and the Russians could blow each other off the map. Mother said the very possibility was what made war unlikely. Then she and the Great Man went into the kitchen to do the dishes. She didn't agree with the Zander method of letting them pile up in the sink until there weren't any left.

Mr. Zander walked out on the porch and leaned on the railing, looking kind of moody. I didn't think he knew I was there, but after a while, he said, "It's been quite a day, hasn't it? Jeeps,

Reds, thunderstorms, war heroes, nuclear holocaust—never a dull moment."

"Yeah," I said. "Did you tell them about the jeep?"

"Did you?"

"No. It would upset Mother."

"It certainly would," he agreed. "But you're okay?"

"Sure I am. I mean, it was scary, but it was interesting."

"Interesting," he murmured. "Watching a grown man lose his temper—"

"—But you didn't! He said that nasty stuff about me, and he called you all sorts of names, and you just hung on, not saying anything, until he . . . he did apologize, didn't he?"

"In a manner of speaking."

"That's pretty impressive. I've never heard of anybody—even Mr. Bartlett—making Jack Weller say he's sorry."

"May it do him good," he said sardonically.

"It probably won't," I said. "He and McCarthy—the only thing you can do about them is stand up to them when they badmouth your friends, until finally somebody censures them for good—right?"

"You'd stand up to McCarthy?" he said, suddenly smiling.

"You bet I would, if he called you a Red."

"Wow," he said. "You're a real friend. I'm honored, Peggy the Intrepid."

Friends with Mr. Zander. Not just kid-and-tolerant-adult, but real friends. Two medals in Berlin and all the glory of the Red Diamonds couldn't have made me prouder. "So am I," I said.

Et in Arcadia Ego

The summer I turned twelve, I learned that Not Fitting In was my permanent condition.

Until then, I'd had hopes. Grownups had assured me that the problem was the other kids, and so it would fade away when they caught up with me. Eventually, said Mother, Elizabeth and Darcy and Jane Eyre and Jo March would become *their* best friends. Eventually, said the Great Man, they'd meet Odysseus and Narcissus and Apollo, and then we'd all be the same. Meanwhile, it was okay—even a kind of Presbyterian virtue—that I didn't know the rules in football, didn't understand why Elvis Presley was such a big deal, and couldn't openly share the Zorro craze because I knew (from Mr. Zander) that Walt Disney was a proto-Fascist. So for most of my years at John Dewey Elementary School, I endured semi-isolation as something temporary.

Then in the spring of sixth grade, my class got a tour of the Junior High we were going to be in next year, and within a week, lots of the girls who'd been happy to play horses or tag had suddenly started talking about boys and dances and lipstick, and even Shirley, who was much too bright to swoon over posters of Guy Williams, proudly showed me that she'd started wearing a bra, as if that were an honor instead of something you didn't mention. And suddenly, I found myself enduring semi-isolation that threatened to be permanent.

I was the third girl in the family. The situation occasioned many fewer comments than it had when I was little, because Pris had followed Liz's example and gotten married, so I was the only one left at home. But occasionally someone still remarked on it at dinner parties, thus calling up one of the favorite family stories. It seems that when the Great Man told his mother that a baby was to be born into a family with two teenage girls, she said, "Well, if it's a boy, we'll all drink champagne. If it's a girl, we'll eat a sour pickle." Of course I'd been welcome anyway, Mother would say quickly as guests laughed—and the Great Man would add that Vermont had turned me into as good a son as a man could wish for.

Clearly, the status of only son was one I could not forego—especially since I agreed with the Great Man and Mr. Zander, who sneered at the makeup, self-conscious giggling, and fake dumbness girls thought made them attractive to men. No, I was going to stay a boy/girl, admiring Mr. Rochester, Darcy, Mowgli, Odysseus, Achilles, and Mr. Zander. At the top of my admiration list, though, was Mr. Bartlett, who never raised his voice but was a war hero who was so strong he could throw a hay bale to the top of a loaded truck or pick up a sledgehammer by the end of its shaft and raise it straight to the side. He would have been my role model, but that couldn't be: the teacher who had introduced us to the concept and asked us to identify our role models had divided the blackboard into two columns, one for boys and one for girls. I'd chosen Mrs. Bartlett, but even that was shocking in a list otherwise limited to Shirley Temple, Judy Garland, and Annette Funicello. And when I remarked that the girls' column didn't look like much compared to the boys' lists of baseball and football stars, drummers, presidents, generals, and movie actors, one of the popular girls giggled and said that a farmer's wife wasn't going to change that, so I shut up.

Anyway, Mr. Bartlett was my hero, and I'd been the happiest

kid in Vermont the summer I turned ten, because the Great Man had bought a 1940 Ford tractor just like Mr. Bartlett's, except it came with an eight hundred pound rotary brush hog. Mother was sure the Great Man would grind himself up, but I was as excited as he was, so we formed a United Front and finally she let me join him, sitting precariously on the fender while he forced it into the overgrown fields behind the house. It was like riding a dragon, complete with smoke from the Great Man's cigarette; it bumped and bucked, and sometimes the weight of the brush hog pulled the front wheels off the ground and you had to steer with the brakes while, with terrible crunches and grinding, the huge blades devoured the bushes and little trees that were crowding out the grass. The bushes didn't grow back, but the grass did, just the way Mr. Bartlett said it would, and our fields slowly became *real* fields. Last summer, when Mr. Bartlett had fenced them for his heifers, they'd looked the way Vermont should.

This summer, however, my new consciousness of the difficulty of being a boy/girl made me aware that I didn't like the tractor the way real boys and men did. When it broke down, which was pretty often, I lost interest just as the Great Man got most involved with it. He explained how things should work, but while I could pretend enthusiasm and fetch tools, I knew I wasn't nearly as good a tractor companion for him as Mr. Zander or even Rob Bartlett, who *enjoyed* lying in the dirt and staring up at a maze of indistinguishable oily parts that should have worked and refused to.

It was the same with baseball. For years, I'd been the only girl allowed to play with the boys at recess, and one of the proudest moments of my life had occurred when I was second baseman with a runner trying to steal from first, and the guys on his team shouted "Get back! Get back! Peggy can catch!" He'd just laughed—until I *did* catch, and tagged him out. But baseball itself . . . well, I enjoyed going to the summer games in Vermont, where there were hot dogs and potato salad on card tables covered with oil cloth, and everybody knew everybody. But the boys in my class listened to baseball, talked about the World Series, traded baseball cards—all things that as a boy/girl I should like but didn't. The situation at school made me realize I was at best only almost as good as a boy, but no good as a girl, a thought so dispiriting that I ignored it for the last weeks of sixth grade.

Once we got to Vermont, though, being a boy/girl was still perfectly all right, and I looked forward to a summer of working on my farming skills. Haying season was just starting—looking over the Bartletts' mowing, I could see the tractor stopped in the middle of a square of cut hay—and I planned to go help every day, like Rob and Joan did, so I'd get strong and brown. And at home, the first place the Great Man and I went after we'd unpacked was the tractor shed, and as he talked about recharging the battery and changing the oil, I found out I was tall enough to push down the clutch and brakes without standing up, so I could drive it solo.

That was such great news I just *had* to share it, so I left the Great Man fussing with wires and jumper cables and walked the half mile to the Bartletts', stopping now and then to say hello to the goldfinches and thrushes that lived on the sunny hill up to their house. It was late in the day, and as I climbed the hill past the mowing, the light was golden in the swaying grass. That meant it was milking time, and I walked a little faster, hoping I'd be in time to go find the cows with Joan and Rob and Rex. As I turned into their yard, I looked back and saw our house on the opposite hill, surrounded by fields instead of brush, and decorated by the long shadows of trees. Except for the view from our house, it was the most beautiful scene in the world.

When I turned around and walked further into the Bartletts' dooryard, though, I got an eerie feeling, because it was awfully quiet for this time of day. It wasn't too surprising that Joan and

Rob weren't there. That just meant I'd missed them—but no, Rex was barking from his chain instead of being with them, and the bars that should have been put across the opening to the dooryard so no cows would trot out to the road weren't in place. I walked behind the upper barn, expecting to see Tommy and Teddy, the work horses, nickering expectantly at the fence, but they were nowhere to be seen. And most mysterious of all, Mr. and Mrs. Bartlett weren't down in the lower barn forking hay into the stanchions. Except for Rex, who had finally recognized me and was whining to be let loose, there was nobody there but me.

If I hadn't known something about farms, I would have gone back home, assuming the Bartletts had gone shopping. But I did know something about farms, and one of those things was that you just *had* to be around at milking time. Unless something was wrong. I looked around, listening to the creepy silence. Then I shouted, "Joan! Joan!"

Nobody answered, but Rex whined and wriggled and pointed his nose up the hill towards the big pasture gate . . . and there were all the cows, who had turned up of their own accord. At the sound of my voice, they bunched up and started trying to get through. I thought of going up there and opening it—they all knew their own stalls, and it would just have been a matter of hitching them up, which I more or less knew how to do. But then I thought about there being no hay ready forked for them, and after that I thought about what Mr. Bartlett would say if one of us kids messed with the cows and something went wrong. So I just stood there, trying to figure out what to do.

Rex pricked up his ears, and I looked the way he was looking, towards the road. Pretty soon, a pickup truck came tooling into the driveway, and out jumped two tired-looking men in overalls. I recognized them instantly as the guys who worked for Mr. Weller, but while I was struggling to remember their names, one of them gave me a surprised look and said, "My gosh—*this* is Peggy?"

The other one shook his head and said, "Grow up fast, don't they?"

Mr. Crawford. That was the first one. So the other was Mr. Wolfson. After the terrible summer of Erma and Prince and Mr. Oldcastle, Mother had told me *never* to talk to Mr. Weller's hired men unless a grownup was around, but sometimes you couldn't take Mother's worries too seriously. Mr. Wolfson was second baseman and Mr. Crawford was shortstop, and they ate with the Bartletts after the games, so I figured they were respectable, though they'd never turn up on a blackboard full of kids' role models. I nodded and smiled and said we'd just gotten here today and I'd come up to say hello to Joan.

The two men looked at each other. Then Mr. Crawford shuffled his feet and said, "She ain't here."

"Yeah," I said. "Nobody's here—except us."

"Right," said Mr. Wolfson. "We're here to do the milkin'. You better git home."

Something was clearly wrong, but I knew better than to ask what. "I could help."

"Yeah?" said Mr. Crawford, with a sarcastic smile. "Like, what could you do?"

I looked him straight in the eye. "I could put up the bars—over there—that keep the cows from wandering into the dooryard. I could go up the hill with Rex—he minds me—and bring down the cows. If you fork hay into the mangers, I can slip the stanchions around the cows' necks. I'm not allowed to use milking machines, but I can show you where they are. And—" I gave him my best we're-all guys-together smile— "I can shovel."

The two men looked at each other. I took advantage of the pause to pick up one of the bars that lay alongside the barn and place it in the posts on each side of the driveway.

As if it were a signal, Rex ran out to the end of his chain, and by the time I had the other bar up, he was bouncing up and down like a yo-yo. I came back and leaned over him. "Okay if we go get the cows now? They know their own stalls—all you have to do is open the barn doors."

The two guys finally moved, and Mr. Crawford muttered, "Heck, let her, if she kin really do it. I gotta git home."

Mr. Wolfson nodded, and the two of them ducked under the bars and started down to the barns.

If she kin really do it. I'd fetched in cows hundreds of times, but as Rex and I climbed the hill, I reflected that Joan and Rob had always been there, keeping the cows from crowding at the gate and running down to the barn, which spoiled their milk. And because it was late, they were pretty het up . . .

It went fine. Rex barked and nipped and organized them, and though they trotted down the hill rather than ambling along, that wasn't unusual, and none of them butted or kicked, so I figured the milk would be okay. I left the gate open at the top, and by the time I'd clambered down the path, all the cows in the upper barn were in the right places, and it was just a matter of the stanchions, which my hands remembered how to do. Mr. Wolfson hustled in with two milking machines just as I'd finished, and he gave me a look that was close to respect.

"You do this a lot?"

I shrugged. "Every time I can. Farming's what I most want to do."

I thought he'd laugh, which grownups generally did when I discussed my ambitions, but instead his face went sad and thoughtful. "Don't look like you'll git the chance," he said. "Hill farmin's jist about gone."

I'd heard that before at baseball games and church suppers, but I'd never thought of it as more than something to complain about. "Bartletts are doing okay," I said.

He shook his head. "Not any more, I reckon. Reason we're

here is Jim had a heart attack mowing this mornin'. Jist had time to shut off the machine before he collapsed."

I stared at him, feeling my legs go numb. "A heart attack! You mean, he's—"

"He warn't dead an hour ago, when Edie called Weller about the milkin'. But they're all at the hospital for the night, 'cause things don't look good." He hitched a milking machine to the first cow.

I swallowed over the desert in my throat. "But why? I mean, Mr. Bartlett's not old and not fat and he doesn't smoke and—"

"—Worry. That's what's done it. Don't know how bad things are, but he lost the old hoss in his team early in sugarin' season. Had to stop, so he was out all that cash, had to sell the other jist to make do, and you don't get much for work hosses these days."

Tommy. The huge, patient horse that had given me so many rides. If I hadn't known that crying would undo Mr. Wolfson's half-respectful glance, I would have burst into tears.

"An' then," he said bitterly, hitching up the second cow, "there's the price of milk. Gone clear down outta sight. Jim was worried jist crazy about how he was gonna make it when it cost him more to keep a herd than he got fer milk. Weller, too, even with his bigger operation. That's why he's thinkin' of—"

"—Chuck!" said Mr. Crawford's voice behind me. "Keep your durnfool trap shut."

Mr. Wolfson's face shifted out of story-telling mode as he ducked behind another cow, but Mr. Crawford still looked cross. "Peggy," he said, "we're real glad for yer help, but there ain't much you kin do now, an' yer folks are gonna wonder where you are."

He knew better than to give me an order, but I knew better than not to recognize this one, because what he said was true. If I stayed until the end of milking, I wouldn't be home for another hour, and I'd probably have to explain, which would lead to another lecture about not associating with Mr. Weller's farm hands. Besides, Mr. Zander was coming for dinner—or rather *with* dinner, which had become a tradition on our first night in Vermont. So I put Rex back on his chain, gave him a scoop of dry dog food and a dish of water, and started home. On my way down the hill, I looked across the mowing at Mr. Bartlett's tractor, stopped in the middle of a row. I didn't cry or anything. I just looked, trying to believe it.

When I turned into our driveway, Mr. Zander's MG had drawn up behind our station wagon, and I could hear the sound of laughter drifting out the kitchen window with delicious whiffs of lasagna. I went in, trying to look cheerful, but when Mr. Zander jumped up and gave me a hug, I felt how energetic and funny and *alive* he was, and for a moment I was terrified I'd lose him, too.

"Hey, Pegaroo," he said, releasing me in a way that made me realize I'd been clinging to him. "What's wrong?"

I swallowed the beginnings of tears. "Mr. Bartlett had a heart attack."

The grownups exchanged shocked looks. Then Mother asked, "Are you *sure*, Peggy?" Which meant, was I making it up—my payment for a lifetime of embellishment.

"Yes, I'm sure," I said. "He was mowing, and he just had time to shut off his tractor. That's why it's still standing in the middle of the field."

The Great Man put down his cigarette with an odd little thump, and he and Mr. Zander hustled outside with Mother's bird glasses to take a look across the valley. Mother put down the silverware she'd been holding as if it were too heavy. "Who told you this?"

"There were . . . people . . . there, doing the milking. They said Mrs. Bartlett had called from the hospital."

"Thank heaven they *got* him to the hospital!" She started setting the table as the two men came back in, having confirmed the position of the tractor. "Peggy says he's in the hospital, so he's going to be all right."

That was *not* what I'd said, but I was doing my best not to disclose my source of information, so I kept quiet, except to shake my head once when Mr. Zander looked at me.

"You know," he said gravely, "we can probably find out how he's doing by calling Ida." Ida was the lady who sat at the switchboard downtown and plugged in everybody's phone calls. I'd been told *very strictly* that I should never bug her for information, but of course with Mr. Zander, who had written a famous novel, it was different.

He walked down the hall and gave the phone box a crank. "Ida? Karl Zander here, wondering how Jim . . oh. I see. God. What a . . . right, right. Well, look, tell Edie the Hamiltons are up, and I'm up, and we'll do what we can. Casserole chain? Sure—just give us a date. Bless you, Ida."

In the little silence after he hung up, Mother and the Great Man looked at each other, and I could see Mr. Zander didn't have to tell us what Ida had told him. If I'd been a kid, I'd have sidled up to Mother for a hug, but since I was too old for that kind of stuff, I just stood there, noting how gray and sad Mr. Zander's face was as he walked back into the kitchen.

"Apparently it was massive," he said, sitting down heavily. "Nothing they could do."

The Great Man shook his head. "It's unbelievable. Did you ever see him muscle out a sledge hammer? A man like that, active, energetic . . . and still in his thirties, right?"

"Ida says thirty-seven," said Mr. Zander. "Which makes sense: two years after high school in the Service, back to the family farm at twenty, married with two kids by twenty-five . . ." He sighed. "He's the first of the last to go."

"He's what?" I said.

"I mean he's the first to die of the tiny generation of farmers who came back to Vermont after the War."

Suddenly I was in the upper barn loft, cuddling a kitten after the storm, and Mr. Bartlett was talking about the ruined land he'd seen in France. *Seeing all them places, I jist wanted to come home an' farm.* "He was *right* to come back!" I said tearfully.

"He sure was," said Mr. Zander, in a voice that somehow let me know he was thinking of that afternoon, too. "But there were plenty of other farmers in office jobs like mine, which means the army introduced them to indoor bathrooms, running water, heat that came on when you turned a dial, steady work—and they left for the city or the suburbs." He gave me a sad smile. "That's why your fields are grown over and you have barn cellars to play in instead of barns."

The Great Man said something about land prices, and the two of them were off about the new ski area, which had tripled the value of Mr. Zander's farm but threatened to surround him with condominiums and motels, but I was only half listening. Because what Mr. Zander said about the barn cellars and fields had popped a kind of balloon in my mind, and I was staring at what was left. Like my status of boy/girl, the popped balloon had Not Fitting In scribbled across its shriveled remains. I'd made the balloon when I'd been little, imagining a life of a me that was really a Bartlett (with minor adjustments for the Great Man, Mother, and Grammy); and I'd created a life for that imaginary me out of things I'd never actually done, though they were based on things I had—like bringing in the cows and haying and halter-breaking calves. What I realized, sitting in the kitchen and looking out the window at the brush and second-growth trees, was that I hadn't actually lived that life, and that outside my imagination Vermont wasn't a golden world where it was always summer, but a place that drove farmers away to the kind of life I found so dull—and where war heroes who'd stayed loyal to their fields, barns and cows died of worry. *"Hill farmin's jist about gone."*

Someone enclosed my shoulders in a hug, and as I jerked myself back into the kitchen, Mother was saying "—very difficult for her."

I leaned against her for a second before pushing her away. "Difficult for *me?*" I said, more rudely than I intended, "Why aren't you thinking about *them? They're* the ones—"

"—Peggy, keep your voice down," said Mother. "Of course we're worried about them, and we'll go over first thing tomorrow to see what we can do."

"I'll come too," said Mr. Zander. "Bet they can use all the help they can get—right, Peggy?"

"Sure," I said. But as we sat down to eat, I reflected that first thing in the morning meant ten o'clock for us, by which time the Bartletts would have been up for five or six hours, and that *none* of them had realized the most important thing they could do was the milking. Milking, with its quiet barn, meditatively munching cows, chugging machines, and expectant cats had no place in their Vermont. As I listened to them turn the conversation to the Great Man's latest translation and Mr. Zander's new novel, I realized with dreadful clarity that the world I was supposed to fit into was not the Bartletts', but theirs.

Ω

For the next few days, every time I began to slip back into the storybook balloon I'd been living in since I was five, remembering that Mr. Bartlett was dead popped it all over again. What made me finally stop that slipping was the funeral, which happened at the end of the week. There were two parts to it. The first was the viewing, and what was viewed was Mr. Bartlett, laid out in a coffin in a suit and tie. The viewers were the Bartletts' friends and family, who came to the funeral home to "pay their respects," which the women did by sitting around the coffin and crying, and the men did by sitting in the next room, smoking and talking about Mr. Bartlett, the baseball team, haying, planting, and tractors.

Standing in the doorway between the two rooms, I saw in a way I'd never seen before that Not Fitting In wasn't just my problem. The Great Man knew a fair number of the men; Mother knew a fair number of the women. But though we'd been friends with the Bartletts all these years, we didn't belong there. We were dressed differently. We talked differently. And while everybody was friendly, they were also honored—honored!—that we'd come. As if we were better than all these people who worked so hard, when all we did was a little gardening and mowing. I had to wonder why I'd never noticed that before.

And then, there was the painful way the set-up accentuated my boy/girl status. I really wanted to hear what the men were saying, and just by glancing in I could see how kind they were being to Rob in an understated way. But Mother shepherded me into the room with the women, and for a moment, my sorrow for Mr. Bartlett was eclipsed by the vision of Joan. Not the Joan I'd known for seven years. A Joan out of *Seventeen*, with lipstick, pancake makeup, eye shadow. A Joan whose straight mousy brown hair was tinted red and rolled into fashionable curls. A Joan dressed in a flower-print shirtwaist in the latest style and sandals with little heels. I sat next to her, of course, and I tried to say I was sorry. But though I could see she was really upset about her father, she was trying not to cry so her makeup wouldn't smear, and when she looked at me, I could *feel* her thinking that I was still a kid, and she'd grown up.

The second part of the funeral was better. For one thing, it was at the cemetery, which overlooked the river, with mountains in the distance—the kind of place you'd like to be buried in. There were a *lot* of people there, including Mr. Zander, and you could tell that although Mr. Bartlett was always so quiet, I wasn't the only one in town who admired him. The coffin was draped in a flag, and the guys who carried it from the hearse to the grave were all in uniform. Another man in uniform—a fancy one with lots of bars and medals and things on it—talked a little about how much Mr. Bartlett had given his country, and how many soldiers had been saved because he'd risked his own life to take care of them. The preacher read a service that made me think of Grammy, with lines in it like "The Lord giveth and the Lord taketh away," and "Ashes to ashes, dust unto dust." The soldiers took the flag from the coffin, folded it, and gave it to Mrs. Bartlett. Then they lowered Mr. Bartlett slowly into the grave while a bugler played Taps. A lot of men saluted or took off their hats, and I cried silently, the way I had when Grammy died.

Taps was so beautiful. Mr. Bartlett had been so wonderful. And I was going to be so lonely without his world.

This Is the Way the Ladies Ride

I reached puberty at the same time Mother reached menopause. For the next two years, each day found one—or more usually, both—of us in tears. The Great Man withdrew to his study and his verse translation of Ovid's *Metamorphoses*.

If it had been just a matter of hormones—the inexplicable gore, the chills, the cramps, the shame of disposing Kotex in the girls' bathroom—I could have borne the disgusting cross of adolescence in silence. But the monthly inconvenience was nothing compared to a life overwhelmed by maternal disapproval. It blew my mind, if you really want to know. For years, though Mother had worried about my penchant for embellishing the truth, I had been able to count on her being sensible and supportive about other things. Now, all of a sudden, she'd become an unrelenting critic—and all, she assured me tearfully, for the sake of my future happiness.

Months of defensive inattention to lectures, snapped comments, and despondent remarks finally led me to understand that her idea of my future had nothing to do with the one I worried about—next week in school, next summer in Vermont, next year in ninth grade. What distressed her was the prospect of my womanhood, which was apparently going to be blighted by my refusal to adopt appropriately ladylike behavior. Since part of a lady's behavior consisted of letting people guess what they were doing wrong instead of telling them, I had a hard time finding a general principle behind individual reproaches until the day I came home from after-school Chess Club and found Mother surrounded by dishes from a Monday Club luncheon.

"Hey, guess what!" I said, picking up a dishtowel. Then, looking at her more carefully, I added, "Are you okay?"

"Of course," she said, with the smile that said she was not okay but we were to pretend she was. I'd seen a lot of that smile. After we'd returned from Vermont last summer, she'd spent a week in the hospital for what she insisted was just a checkup. I had not been fooled—a checkup did not require two months' convalescence, a flurry of phone calls from Liz and Pris, or constant, frantic attendance from the Great Man—but as the subject was not open for discussion, I'd learned to appear oblivious. Still, there were limits to what even I could be expected not to notice.

"Maybe you should sit down and let me make you a cup of tea," I suggested.

She hesitated, then to my surprise she sat heavily on a kitchen chair. To forestall the tears that were obviously pending, I put the kettle on and started washing, but I was not surprised when she broke the silence.

"Just look at all this mess! I just can't seem to handle it anymore."

I was tempted to say that I would have come home two hours earlier if she'd asked me to help, but she would have taken it as a criticism, so I changed the subject. "It's the beginning of the Chess Club tournament. I thought I'd have to start way at the bottom, since I'm only an eighth grader, but Mr. McAffee ranked me with Joe Strangeways—he's the best of the juniors."

Mother's smile became a real one. "Oh—I heard about that tournament! Joe's mother was here today. She expected him to go to the top. Apparently he's very good."

"Yes he is," I said, giving her the promised cup of tea. "But he's not going to the top. I beat him two games out of three."

Her cup clinked against its saucer as I turned back to the sink. "You did *what?*"

"I beat the socks off him," I said, not without pleasure. "He's brilliant and flamboyant, but he ignores details. It's just a matter of waiting for him to make mistakes." I began drying the plates in the rack, a little hurt at her silence. It wasn't until I turned to put them away that I realized that somehow I'd goofed again.

"Peggy," she said, her voice quivering, "you can't go on this way."

"You're right," I said, brusquely stashing the plates in the cupboard. "I'm supposed to play Marv Kaplan next, and he'll cream me. Unless he leaves me an opening, of course."

"There's satisfaction in seeing an opening and not taking it."

I stared at her. "You mean, you're saying I should let them beat me?"

"You'll find yourself in such situations often as you grow up," she said. "If you want to keep on playing with boys, you'll have to learn subtle strategies of competition. The point is to play as well as you can, but ignore mistakes that would let you win, so they appreciate your skill as an opponent without seeing you as a threat."

"You *are* saying I should let them beat me!"

"Not in such a way that they notice you're doing it. That actually takes more skill than winning."

"So men are such children that they can't take an honest defeat!"

"Peggy," said Mother, "Let me tell you a story. Long ago, I became one of the best writers in my college. I wanted to become a great novelist, so when your father and I got engaged and he started to apply to graduate schools, I wanted to apply, too—a very daring move back in 1930." Her eyes came back from the window to be sure I was listening, but for once, I was listening very closely indeed. Her occasional absorption in her writing was another thing I wasn't supposed to notice, but I knew her novels were good enough to interest the Great Man. There was a box of them in the attic, all neatly typed on yellow paper and filed in manila folders.

"So," Mother continued, "I went to Dr. Oliver, who was my favorite English teacher as well as dean of the College, and I asked him for a recommendation." She sipped her tea, and I thought of her yearbook, which I'd found one day in a box next to the novels. It opened to a half-page picture of her as "Class Beauty." Her face had been too other-worldly for the Roaring Twenties, or even for stuffier 1960; but she'd been beautiful, all right.

"Did Dr. Oliver say you were too pretty for grad school?"

"No," she said. "He said, 'Ellen, you're engaged to a brilliant young man with magnificent prospects. But to go as far as Ned's capable of going, he'll need the kind of devoted wife Emily has been to me all these years. By following your own career, you will make it impossible to devote yourself to him; and your marriage, like those of other couples with two careers, will almost certainly fail. This is not to discourage you; you're very talented. But before you apply, take a day to consider the problems that attend ambition.'"

"Don't tell me you let him stop you!" I said indignantly.

"Of course not. I stopped myself. I realized that being competitive is acceptable in a girl, but that becoming a woman involves sacrificing personal ambition to family happiness."

"What if you don't have a family?" I asked. "I mean, look at Mr. Zander—he doesn't have a wife supporting him all the time, and he's famous."

"Mr. Zander has decided not to marry several bright women he's dated seriously."

"*He* said one week in Vermont with them made him realize they had no inner resources. That's boredom, not competition!"

"No man *admits* he can't take competition."

"Okay, so he's lying. But the point is, he's successful *without* a sacrificial—"

"—We're not talking about Mr. Zander," she said. "We're talking about competing, which is something a woman does at her peril. Being supportive, tactful, and understanding is as much a part of womanhood as good manners and graciousness."

"And what does that supportive, tactful, understanding woman end up with?" I asked, feeling my temperature rise.

"Don't worry," she said soothingly. "There are many rewards, as you'll find."

"I can hardly wait! All I have to do is grow up, stop competing, let men win . . . and I'll become the perfect Monday Club lady! God damn!"

Mother sat up straight, her exhausted face filled with shock. "Peggy, that kind of language is not appropriate in this house."

"The hell you say!" I threw the dishtowel across the kitchen and stomped out.

I was still shaking when I got to the top of the stairs. I turned into my room and slammed my book bag on the bed, wishing I hadn't demolished my punching bag years ago so I could do it now. It didn't help that I knew that my comment on Monday Club ladies had been tactless . . . even cruel. Or that I couldn't forget that Mother's once-beautiful face was gray with pain. Or that I'd only done half the dishes.

I absolutely could not go back down there and do the damn things. But as my sobs quieted and my ears stopped ringing, I heard the familiar clicking of the Great Man's typewriter. Maybe . . . yeah. I washed my face, tiptoed to his study, knocked quietly, and opened the door.

The smoke was so thick I could hardly see him, though the room, which had been Grammy's back in the days before all this ladylike behavior stuff had hit me, wasn't very big. He looked up benignly as I coughed. "You want to know something interesting?" he said. "It's about Tiresias."

"The guy who could see the future through cigarette smoke?"

He laughed. "It is a little thick in here, isn't it? But listen— just before the story of Echo and Narcissus, there's one of those nifty passages that lets you know Ovid is a master psychologist. It begins with a semi-dirty joke . . ." He trailed off with a worried frown—dirty jokes were inappropriate in our house.

"Of course it does," I said encouragingly. "How could it be genuine Ovid if it didn't?"

He looked relieved. "Okay—Ovid tells us Jove and Juno were arguing about who had more fun in bed: Jove said women; Juno said men. They agreed to consult Tiresias, because once, Tiresias had seen two snakes mating, attacked them with a stick— and turned into a woman. Then seven years later, Tiresias the woman had caught two snakes at it *again*—and she'd attacked them—and bingo! She'd re-become a man."

I nodded appreciatively, wondering how snakes did it, anyway.

"So," he went on, "Jove and Juno knew Tiresias could answer their question from firsthand experience. But when they called him in, he said women definitely had more fun in bed than men. That made Juno so angry that she struck him blind . . . but Jove apologetically gave him the power to see Truth." He stubbed out the cigarette that had been in his hand, along with a couple he'd left burning aimlessly in his ashtray. "Now, think what that means, metaphorically speaking." He paused, but I knew enough not to guess. "It means that real understanding, real insight into events and people, belongs to somebody who is male *and* female. Which in turn means that the gender you're born into *limits your vision*. True understanding is androgynous. Isn't that amazingly perceptive?"

"It sure is," I said. "But where does that leave us?"

He laughed. "Little pragmatist! Listen, has the Monday Club left yet?"

"It left quite a while ago. Mother's downstairs with this enormous pile of dishes."

"Hell's bells!" he said, jumping up. "I told her I'd do them. Why didn't she——?"

"She's pretty tired." His sharp look made me think I might be treading on dangerous territory, so I added, "I was helping for a while, but then she got upset because I beat Joe Strangeways in the chess tournament."

"The Strageways boy? His father says he's very good. Look, let's have a game this evening." He patted me on the shoulder as he hurried out the door.

Ω

Tiresias became my role model. Michigan was short on mating snakes, but after I'd figured out how to spell "androgynous" and looked it up, I found it was more or less what I wanted, so I settled for that. Instead of submitting to Mother's hairdresser's weekly attempts to give me "soft curls," I went to the Great Man's barber and got a "pixie," in which no hair was longer than four inches. With mental apologies to Grammy, I accustomed my tongue to the expletives used by the boys a couple of classes ahead of me. And after a lifetime of indifferent academic performance, I decided to be better than everybody at everything—and was rewarded by the highest grade-point in my class, the sub-editorship of the literary magazine, and the vice-presidency of the Chess Club.

That summer in Vermont, I dressed only in jeans and un-tucked army shirts, kindly bequeathed to me by Pris's husband. Initially I went barefoot, but I hastily donned riding boots after Mr. Zander asked if I was becoming a Beatnik. He laughed at my "middle class stuffiness," but later I overheard him tell the Great Man that the Prussian cavalry officer look became me. The Great Man, to my surprise, agreed.

The chief news Mr. Zander brought us upon our arrival was that Mr. Weller had sold his farm—650 acres, houses, barns, fields, maple groves, sugar houses—to a rich guy from out of state who wanted a healthy atmosphere for his daughter and a tax loss. Town rumor had it that Mr. Weller had asked forty thousand dollars, but the rich guy had gone to his house one evening with thirty-five thousand dollars in one hundred dollar bills and counted them out and Mr. Weller had been unable to resist. "But there's no getting the best of Weller," said Mr. Zander. "He agreed to the sale only on the condition that he become foreman. So he has moved into the smaller house, which he gets rent free, and he gets a salary whether the farm makes money or not, AND he puts thirty-five grand into the bank."

"You have to admire his cunning," said the Great Man, laughing. "My grandfather—the racehorse breeder Peggy looks so much like—would have liked him."

"What's our new neighbor's name?" asked Mother.

"Rockefeller," said Mr. Zander—and savored the disbelief in our faces. "No, I'm kidding. His name is George Hapney, but his wife is a Rockefeller, which is where the money comes from. Or so they say. I met them at the Dunning's Supply, looking over garbage cans—handsome, polite capitalists-turned-estate-owners. And—" he glanced at me— "their daughter is a bit older than you, goes to Miss Porter's in the winter, but in the summer shows her horse. Unfortunately, she's in trouble at Miss Porter's—not sure why, but I've heard that dyslexia runs parallel to money in the Rockefeller bloodlines—so she has to go to summer school. Which means she's desperately looking for somebody to exercise her horse so she can continue to win trophies."

"You're kidding!" I said.

Mother gave him a reproachful look. "Don't get all excited, Peggy. Show horses can be very spirited. They may need somebody far more experienced than you are."

I almost retorted that it wasn't my fault I wasn't more experienced than I was, but I didn't want to argue in front of Mr. Zander. Besides, Mother's remark, though founded in fear, was truer than she knew. In Michigan, I had watched my cranky, elderly riding teacher draw beautiful dressage out of the cranky, elderly horse that I could barely keep in a canter. It was a lesson in humility.

But the seed was sown, and the next afternoon, when the Great Man was fussing with his tractor and Mother was taking a nap, I strolled down to what I still thought of as Mr. Weller's farm. For a while, the walk looked just the way it always had . . . "always" of course meaning since the Oldcastles' house and barn had burned down. In six years the foundations had faded into the landscape, with raspberries flourishing in the rotting barn beams and brambly roses sprawling over the house's old retaining wall. But once I'd rounded the corner, the territory became oddly unfamiliar. The fences that had lined the road in Mr. Weller's day had been straggly stone walls with posts shoved into them and held more or less vertical by rusty barbed wire. Now the old walls were gone, and the fence was made of wire in four-inch squares, four feet high, held upright by deeply-driven metal posts and topped with the cleanest, meanest barbs I'd ever seen. The gate, when I came to it, wasn't the old one with bars of half-grown maples, but a huge metal rectangle hung from one specially-braced post, chained to another, and padlocked. Looking over it, I could see that the fence went all the way around the pasture. Twenty acres, maybe thirty. An unfamiliar, worldly voice in my mind whispered that a fence like that must be expensive.

I walked on, marveling at the new paint job and enlarged porch on the Big House that had been Mr. Weller's, when somebody shouted "Hey, Peggy!" I turned around and saw Mr. Wolfson standing in the barn door, looking as tired and scruffy as ever. I knew we weren't supposed to converse, but he helped the Bartletts with haying and planting when he could, and that made us friends.

"Hi," I said, walking up the ramp. "Good to see ya."

"Yup." He waved his hand at the painted Big House, the new roof on the Little House, the glistening red truck in the driveway, and the new fence around the mowing. "What'cha think?"

I shrugged. "Pretty fancy. Is Mr. Hapney okay to work for?"

"Good enough. Fair-minded. Fixes things."

"Great." I hoped the fixing extended to the house Mr. Wolfson and his family had been renting from Mr. Weller. It wasn't as bad as the Oldcastles', but it was pretty run down. "I heard he has a daughter about my age."

"Older," he said emphatically. "Eighteen, prob'ly. She ain't comin' up 'til the weekend, but her hoss is here. You wanna see?" He pushed himself off the doorjamb and started down to the pen behind the barn where Mr. Weller's cows had gathered at milking time. I followed, but when we turned the corner I stopped and stared.

The old pen was gone. In its place—well, more than in its place, because somehow they'd made it four times as big—was a grassy paddock surrounded by a white board fence, and beyond that, a riding ring. Standing in the paddock was a liver chestnut Morgan mare with an intelligent face.

Mr. Wolfson looked at me over his shoulder. "Like it?"

"Yeah," I said. "But . . . I mean . . . he just bought the place in March, right? How'd he get grass like this?"

"Fill. Bulldozer. Big wall on the far side. Fifteen workin' here, top count. Then sod—you know, unrolled from a truck, give it coupl'a weeks, you got Kentucky bluegrass right here in Vermont." He spat to one side. "You shoulda seen Weller's face.

Showed him what *real* money kin do."

It had never occurred to me that money—even real money—could change a landscape. I looked uncertainly at Mr. Wolfson. "Do *you* like it?"

He scratched his stubbly chin in a way incongruous with the backdrop. "Wal, it looks smart, y'know. An' a man's gotta right to do what he wants with his own land."

"I guess so." I watched the mare stick her lovely head over the fence. "May I pat her?"

"Sure. She likes to be scratched right here." He rubbed her behind the ears, and she moved her head up and down appreciatively.

"I didn't know you liked horses," I said.

"My uncle deals hosses," he said. "You prob'ly seen him around. Small, plaid shirt, beret—Joe the Frenchman, they call him, 'cause of that hat." He looked sideways at me. "An 'cause he was a loggin' accident with a Frenchie's daughter."

That was obviously a joke, so I laughed knowingly, which enabled me not to say that at Green Mountain Stables, where I rode in the summer, Joe the Frenchman's reputation was less than savory.

Mr. Wolfson must have seen something in my face, because he added, "'Course, Joe never gits a quality hoss like this. But he has an eye for what's under rough coats and ribs. If you buy a hoss from Joe, you kin ride it." He watched me scratch the mare under the chin. "Y'know, Miss Eighteen's gonna need somebody to exercise this lady."

I nodded in what I hoped was a non-committal way. "She a lot of trouble?"

"The hoss?" He laughed. "You jist sit there and push her buttons. The girl, well . . ."

Behind us, a horn sounded a long beep—Mr. Weller's signal for action. Mr. Wolfson hustled back up to the barn, and by the time I got there, he and Mr. Weller were loading scrap lumber into the new truck. Mr. Weller said it was good to see we were back; I admired the truck, and then I walked home along the new fence, wondering what a girl whose father could change landscapes would be like.

Ω

She was beautiful.

I didn't know much about feminine embellishment, but even I could see that the swept-back hair, the eye shadow, and the lipstick enhanced her natural scenery—tall, blond, slim, graceful. Mr. Zander, who saw her walk up the drive just as he was about to send my croquet ball into the swamp, muttered "Holy Jesus!" and muffed the shot.

Mother rose from the Adirondack chair to greet her (and her parents, who were there but you didn't notice at first). "You must be the Hapneys," she said with her best gracious smile.

Introductions were performed. The girl was Sarah; the parents were Henry and Mary. They'd be delighted to sit for a minute—no, no tea, thank you. Peggy would fetch her father from his study—no, no bother at all. And it turned out not to be. The Great Man, though a little surly at my interruption, was so stricken by Sarah that he could hardly keep his eyes off her.

After a quarter hour of social niceties, during which Sarah and Mrs. Hapney talked to Mother, Mr. Hapney talked to the Great Man and Mr. Zander, and I remained silent, Mrs. Hapney opened the shopping bag that had been the only unaccountable thing in her perfect get-up and drew out an album. "Weller tells us that Peggy is a rider," she said, smiling at me. "We brought some pictures of Sarah and her horse, Windcrest Dolly."

Mother smiled apprehensively; the Great Man looked at best tolerant. Neither of them realized that "Windcrest" should evoke the same reaction as "Rockefeller." But the pictures told them what they should have known. Sarah, straight and elegant in full riding habit, rode with her hands held high; Dolly, trotting with her neck perfectly arched and her mane flying, lifted her feet so high her forearms were parallel to the ground. A few pictures later, Dolly stood in a perfect stretch as Sarah accepted an enormous trophy.

Mr. Hapney smiled proudly at the picture. "Sarah was junior champion at the National Morgan Horse Show last year," he said. "She won *every* class."

"It really was gratifying," said Mrs. Hapney. "She'd worked very hard. But this summer, she'll only be able to ride on weekends, so we were very happy to learn that there was a girl down the road who might be able to help us out."

I glanced at Sarah, wondering how she felt about being talked about as if she were absent; but like her parents, she was looking at Mother and the Great Man. The Great Man looked at me dubiously. "Peggy, do you ride this way?"

"Not at *that* level, you can bet," I said . . . and paused in confusion as all three men snickered. "I mean," I amended, "I've only ridden saddle seat a little, because my lessons in Michigan are hunt seat and in Vermont I ride whatever way the horse goes best. But I know the saddle seat signals."

"Wonderful!" said Mr. Hapney, turning to the Great Man. "Could she come ride Dolly this afternoon, so Sarah could show her the ropes? We have to leave at five."

We all went—including Mr. Zander, who was unnaturally quiet. When we got there, Mr. Weller pointed to the arena behind the barn, grinning in a way that puzzled me until I saw Mr. Wolfson finish saddling Dolly and lead her to the ring where Sarah waited.

"Thank you, Wolfson," she said, giving him a lovely smile. "Now, Peggy, before you mount, make her stretch—like this."

She held the reins closely under Dolly's chin; Dolly immediately froze in perfect position. I patted her and started to change the stirrup length, and as I glanced at Sarah to judge how many holes they should go up, I caught the last look I had expected to see in that perfect face: the narrowed eyes of someone sizing up the competition.

Somehow that look took me out of the unfamiliar world that had been making me uneasy. I swung on, gathered the double reins with a familiarity gained from riding a hard-mouthed gelding the previous summer, and nudged Dolly towards the rail. Walk, trot, walk. Halt. She halted, but I felt her confusion and realized that her push buttons worked only for a straight saddle-seat routine. So we'd stick with that. Walk, canter. Reverse. Same drill, without the halt. She was so eager to please me that after we'd done figure eights at a trot and canter and finished with a perfect stretch in the center, I leaned forward and hugged her.

"Bravo!" "Good work!" came voices from the rail. Looking over my shoulder as I dismounted, I was surprised to see so many people. My parents and Mr. Zander, of course, and the Hapneys—but Mr. Wolfson and Mr. Weller were standing a bit behind them, and so was a little man in a black beret. I led Dolly towards Sarah, who wasn't looking quite as happy as I'd hoped. It was time to let her show off.

"She's a sweetheart," I said. "I wish I could make her move as beautifully as you do. Will you show me how?"

She swung on—and within seconds Dolly ceased to be sweetly willing and became professional, spectacular, spirited. As she thundered by, Mr. Zander nudged me. "Do all Morgans lift their knees so high?"

I shook my head. "It takes weighted shoes, plus a rider who knows what to ask for."

On my other side, the Great Man stared and stared. "Metamorphosis," he muttered. "A triumph of art over nature."

Ω

When we got home, I expected a maternal lecture on the Perfection of Sarah's Ladylike Manners, but I didn't get one. Or anything else. Mr. Zander and I finished our croquet match (I lost), and later the Great Man joined us for another, and everybody was so busy pretending nothing had happened that when Mr. Zander left, I walked him to his MG.

"Okay," I said. "Tell me what's up."

He wiped a piece of lint off the mirror. "About the horse? She's great. Lucky you."

"Don't bullshit me. Everybody's upset, including you."

"Perceptive Peggy," he said. "It's not the horse, directly. It's . . . it's . . ."

"The money? The manners?"

"Ah. So you noticed."

"How dumb do you think I am? 'Thank you, Wolfson'— Jesus H. Christ!"

He shook his head, half smiling. "Then perhaps you also noticed that to your new neighbors, Weller, the Wolfsons, the Bartletts, you, your parents, me—we're all part of the huge class that waits on them. The lesser gentry, the tenants, the local farmers, the servants— the walk-on parts in Jane Austen."

For a second I got side-tracked, because I'd never thought about Jane Austen that way.

He was looking at me very hard. "See why we're not happy?"

"Sure. By riding Dolly, I become the same sort of servant as Mr. Wolfson and Mr. Weller, right?"

"You got it."

"Well, don't worry," I said, shrugging. "The Hapneys are richer than we are, but we're still gentry, and I'm being brought up to be a lady. So there's no danger that anybody who *matters* will confuse me with Mr. Weller or Mr. Wolfson or—"

"—Jesus, Peggy!"

"Well," I said, "you talk about class and inequality all the time. How can you do that and expect me not to notice what's right in front of me?"

"'You taught me language; and my profit on't is, I know how to curse,'" he muttered. "Look, the whole issue of class is extremely complicated and hard to—"

"—Don't bother," I snapped. "I'll figure it out."

"Okay, go ahead," he said, vaulting into his car. "Good luck."

His expression told me I'd been ruder than I'd intended; so did the way he spun out before I had time to apologize. But he waved as he reached the corner, and I waved back.

Ω

I rode Dolly every weekday between mid-June and Fourth of July weekend, which was the date of the National Morgan Horse Show. I loved grooming her, but since I was allowed to ride only in the ring, and since I was afraid of doing anything that would mess with her push buttons, riding her was boring. On the Friday of the show, a fancy horse trailer turned up in front of the Big House, and I walked her in, gave her a carrot, and struggled to lift the ramp, which became the back door. At the last moment, Mr. Wolfson, who'd been chatting with the driver, came to my rescue, and we bolted it shut.

"Thank you, Wolfson," I said, grinning.

He looked at me, and in the instant before he realized I was kidding and grinned back, I saw a kind of anger I'd never seen before.

I glanced at the driver, to be sure he hadn't heard—and saw it was Joe the Frenchman. "Hey, Peggy," he said.

I joined Mr. Wolfson as he walked to the window, wondering how you addressed a man with no last name. "Hi," I said. "How far is it to the show?"

"Northampton. Coupl'a hours in this rig. Better git goin'. Big deal—first time this hoss meets the big time."

"Really?" I said, turning to Mr. Wolfson. "But there's those pictures—"

"That was last year. Junior rider. But she's had a birthday, so they've gotta compete against the pros."

"I sure hope Dolly's up to that," I said. "Sarah likes to win."

"She sure does," said Mr. Wolfson, and Joe the Frenchman nodded agreement.

I looked from one of them to the other, but their faces were unreadable.

They were even more unreadable on Tuesday, when I went down to the barn and saw the two of them and Mr. Weller leaning on the paddock fence and watching a thin horse devour the Kentucky blue grass in the paddock.

Everything in me wanted to rush down and ask, "Hey, where's Dolly?" But Tiresias saved me by pointing out that if I did that, they'd see me as a kid, and worse, an interfering female. So I made my own face as unreadable as I could, sauntered down the hill, said "Hi," as if nothing had happened, and stepped on the bottom rail of the fence so I could see over it. The three men look at each other uncertainly. Finally, Mr. Wolfson spoke.

"Hapneys said to tell you they won't be needin' you any more, now that they sold Dolly, but they thank you for ridin' her fer them."

"How kind of them to remember the help," I said.

Mr. Weller and Mr. Wolfson laughed outright, and Joe the Frenchman smiled at me. "We was jist sayin' it was a shame you weren't gonna have a hoss to ride."

I nodded. I'd been thinking the same thing; Mother had cancelled my lessons at Green Mountain Stable.

Joe the Frenchman gestured at the horse in the paddock. "How 'bout her?"

I looked at her; she was skin and bone, still shedding her winter coat in blotches. But she was built like the cranky quarter horse thoroughbred cross I rode in Michigan, and she had a sweet face. "Seems like she needs some time off," I said.

"She'll git a week," he said. "Mebbe a bit more. Weller here says we can use the pasture 'til the cattle come. But while she spruces up, I gotta know if she's right fer some folks who're lookin' fer a good kids' hoss. An' that means I need a kid to ride her."

I glanced at Mr. Wolfson, raising my eyebrows.

"Joe," he said, "You gotta tell Peggy—Jake rides every hoss you buy. No broncos."

"'Course," interposed Mr. Weller, "Jake kin keep his seat on anything with four legs an' a tail."

"Would I put this kid in danger?" said Joe. "No, *sir*! I seen her mount up on a fancy Morgan, no fear, and git a good ride outta her, an' I thought, man, she's a *rider*." He turned to me. "So, what you say? You wanna try her out?"

I thought briefly of Mother, involved in the Democratic convention with the confidence that I was riding a reliable horse. It didn't seem right to deal behind her back. On the other hand, any fool could tell that these three men didn't want me to get hurt. I looked at Joe the Frenchman. "Does Jake ride English or Western?"

"Western," he said. "Not her line. Willin' enough, but don't even neck rein. But the family that's interested wants English."

"Okay," I said in my best androgynous voice. "Let's tack her up."

She was so thin I felt guilty putting a saddle on her, but when we got into the ring, she perked up a little. Walk, trot. Halt. I asked for a turn on the forehand, and got it. "Hey," I said as we walked by the men. "Somebody *trained* her! How'd she end up like this?"

"Some kid lost coupl'a classes," said Joe. "Like Miss La-de-da, only this hoss's got no papers, an' there's no daddy to git a fancy price fer her. No buyer, no money for feed—jist left her in the pasture fer the winter. Happens all the time."

I finished the workout with a canter that collected magically when I asked, and stopped her squarely in the center. As I dismounted, she nuzzled my pocket for a carrot, and I gave her one, thinking bitterly of the Unfairness of Things.

"Sweet Jesus," said Joe the Frenchman. "I kin sell her as a lady's mount!"

"Peggy ain't a lady," objected Mr. Wolfson.

"She's lady enough fer me," said Joe.

If I hadn't been drying my tears with the mare's matted mane, it would have been the proudest moment of my life since the catch I'd made on second base, all those years ago.

Watersheds

The summer I turned fifteen, I learned what a watershed was. In school, of course, I'd learned about the Continental Divide, and in conversations with Mr. Zander I'd learned about hackneyed metaphors. But I learned what a watershed *felt like* when Grandmother Hamilton died, and suddenly we had Real Money. Like other family occurrences—Mother's lengthy "checkups" at the hospital in both fall and spring, for example—the inheritance was something we were supposed to live around without discussing. Not realizing that initially, I greeted Pris and her husband with the good news when they arrived in Vermont, and was so roundly scolded for my lack of circumspection that I never mentioned the subject again. Observation, however, qualified as circumspect. Thus, I privately evaluated the amount of Real Money available by estimating the price tags of the new convertible the Great Man bought for Mother, the stereo that replaced our old record player, the electric typewriters that replaced both parents' Remingtons, the flurry of redecoration in the spring, and the tour of Europe that was planned for the fall.

Despite the impressive total I arrived at, I naively thought that while the comfortable shabbiness of the Michigan house was lost to newly-carpeted hardwood floors and painted oak paneling, Vermont would remain untouched. But in late June, a baby grand Steinway replaced the upright that had dominated the Great Man's study, and as it barely left room for his desk, he proposed to make the attached woodshed into a new study—and to build a barn for all the stuff that had piled up in it. I was delighted because, amongst other things, the preliminary sketches of the new barn included a box stall for my horse.

The horse, surprisingly enough, had little to do with Real Money. Towards the end of the previous summer, someone—I suspected Mrs. Hapney—had told Mother that instead of schooling Sarah's Morgan, I had spent two months riding "ladies' mounts" for Joe the Frenchman. The lecture that had followed had been excruciating, my enforced farewell to Joe and Mr. Wolfson had been humiliating, but the result had been the promise of a rented horse for the next summer. And there he was—a solidly built chestnut named Red, whose endearingly patient face and enormous hooves suggested a bar sinister in his purportedly Morgan ancestry. He came with a rough coat and a girth gall that took over a month to heal. Within two weeks, constant grooming had made him shine, and riding bareback had so improved my seat that his benign tricks no longer landed me on the ground.

What Red gave me, beyond a steadfast friend and ally, was a range of movement beyond my wildest imaginings. Though my bike had provided me a degree of freedom in Michigan, my Vermont explorations had been bound by the limitations of my feet or the car. Our car—unlike Rob, Joan, and other local kids, I was instructed, in terms that even I didn't dare ignore, never to accept rides from friends and neighbors. But now, once I'd coaxed Red to the mounting block and vaulted on, I could go anywhere I wanted. And soon, with a map of shortcuts, trails, and secretly spliced fences gradually unfolding in my head, the two of us found our way to places as much as twenty miles away by road.

It was upon returning from one of these rides that I turned off a trail onto our mowing and found the Great Man and my brothers-in-law pacing off the dimensions of the one level spot in the property. Red, of course, was eager to get back to his pasture, but I made him stop while I watched, letting him graze with his bit on as a reward for his patience.

"Just the right size!" said Don (Pris's husband).

"Maybe," said Herb (Liz's husband). "But how much of a drop is that?"

The Great Man turned to the tractor and pulled out the clothesline and a pocket level. "Try these."

Don and Herb looked at him with admiration that must have gratified him. Then Don put his foot on one end of the rope at the highest spot, and Herb walked away, unwinding, until he'd reached the marker they'd put in the grass. The Great Man put his level on the resulting line and shook his head.

"Higher, Herb."

"Sorry," said Herb. "Can't reach any higher."

"God damn," said Don, looking at the triangle between the rope and the ground. "Call it nine feet. That's a helluva lot of fill."

"Well," said Herb, "We can cut out some of the dirt you're standing on, and there's plenty of fill around. Just needs to be gathered."

Fill? Dirt? The time had come to intervene. "What the hell are you doing?" I asked.

They all jumped, but Don smiled. "We're planning a tennis court."

"There're tennis courts downtown!" I said. "Right by the ball field, where the baseball suppers used to happen."

Herb shook his head. "Too short to play a decent game. Spent all yesterday evening running into the fence."

"Um . . . wouldn't it be cheaper just to look out for the fence?"

They laughed, and we started back to the house together.

I thought it was all idle speculation—there had been lots of that about the size and placement of the barn—until I put Red up and came inside. As usual on weekends, Liz and Pris had taken over lunch, which I assembled on weekdays; and also as usual, they made a bigger deal of it than they had to by actually cooking instead of just having sandwiches and fresh stuff from the garden. The food was all set, but everybody was milling around, including Liz's daughter Karen and Pris's daughter Debby, who were starting to whine. I sat them down on either side of me and served them some quiche Lorraine they were unlikely to eat and some bread and jam they started in on right away. That made the men sit down, opening bottles of the imported beer Herb insisted on, and as they made room for Pris and Mother, they were discussing the pros and cons of tennis court types. I was in the midst of learning that playing tennis on cement or asphalt wrecked your knees and spoiled the game when Liz shook my shoulder.

"Peggy, for God's sake, go change! You reek of horse."

Amidst the sudden silence, I looked down at my jeans, which were adorned with the arc of sweat and chestnut hair that came from riding bareback. "It'll be better in a few minutes when they dry," I said helpfully.

Don, Herb, and Pris snickered, and Karen piped up with "She smells fine!"

"Sure," snapped Liz. "Saint Peggy can do no wrong." Then looking at me, "Do you think it's fair to make poor Mother breathe the air around you?"

A glance at Mother told me she was upset—probably not so much about the horsey jeans as about the looming stand-off. So I asked her in my best gracious voice, "Do I have time to change before we're all served?"

She rewarded me with a relieved smile. "Plenty of time, if you hurry."

I scooted upstairs, changed, and got back to my place so fast that dishes were still being passed around. Don was pressing the merits of grass courts, but as he launched into tales of

Wimbledon, the Great Man pointed out the window at the brown lawn.

"We can't even maintain a croquet court," he said. "Two weeks with no rain and that's what happens."

"Of course you'd have to water it—"

"—With what?" I asked. "The well's only six feet deep."

Don frowned. "All the new places they're building at the Mountain have artesian—"

"—Don," said the Great Man in a voice he seldom used, "a tennis court is the *only* extravagance I'm willing to consider."

Anybody but Don would have been shamed to silence, but he just changed tack. "Well, clay is good, too. Take the great clay courts at Deerfield Academy, for example. We could take a spin down there if you'd like to see."

"That won't be necessary," said the Great Man. "Ellen and I saw them when Peggy was taking the Prep School exams. They were quite impressive."

The glance suddenly shared amongst the grownups made me wish he hadn't said that. I'd taken the exams only under duress, and while I'd admired Deerfield's la-de-da campus and marveled at the clerical garb of its intimidating headmaster, I'd steadily resisted hints to think further about my educational opportunities.

"Oh Peggy!" said Pris excitedly. "You're going to go to Bradley?"

"Peggy hasn't made up her mind about applying yet," said Mother quickly.

"Oh, take the plunge!" said Pris. "If they accept you, you can always not go."

Grandmother Hamilton had sent Pris to Bradley Academy for Girls when Liz started going to the University of Michigan. She'd loved it, and everybody said it had gotten her into Radcliffe, which evidently made her education more prestigious than Liz's. But if it had made any difference then, it sure didn't now, because once you got married, all that stuff about schools just turned into something you looked back on nostalgically as the time when you'd had hopes instead of kids.

So I said "Sure," to Pris in as noncommittal a way as I could, and added, with sudden insight born of desperation, "You know who has a clay court?"

"In town?" said Herb.

"Well, in Westover. There's a big Boston family, the Hendersons, who've been summer people since the 1890s, when Mr. Zander's grandfather farmed their property as well as his. And *they* have a tennis court, and Mr. Zander says it's pretty good, but nobody plays on it but them and their guests."

"Are they so exclusive they wouldn't let us look at it?" said Don.

I shrugged. "You could ask Mr. Zander. He plays there all the time."

"'Mr. Zander,'" said Liz as Don and Herb adjourned to the phone. "You still don't call him Karl?"

I shook my head. He'd been Mr. Zander for so long I was sort of stuck with it.

"What happened to the girl he turned up with last time we were here?" asked Pris.

"She went home," said Mother. "Too bad—she was very pretty."

"She was," I said judiciously, "but she wouldn't admit there was a difference between capitalism and democracy; and she wouldn't leave him alone to write."

"Gracious!" said Mother. "How did you find that out?"

"I asked."

Pris and Liz laughed, and Mother said, "Peggy! You *promised* to be more tactful!"

"Mr. Zander prefers straight questions," I said. "He said it was a relief to tell somebody who would understand why 'the conditions were just impossible.'"

"Hrumph!" said Liz. "Sounds like he's waiting for you."

"That's ridiculous," said Mother sharply. "He's old enough to be her—"

"—brother, in this family," said Liz. "He's only a bit older than I am. So . . ."

"Oh, cut it out!" I said, and she did, because the kids started howling over some squabble, and Herb and Don trooped in to say they were going to Karl's house and from thence to the court. The Great Man, though invited to go with them, declined politely and escaped to his study. After I finished the dishes, I was about to take off for the treehouse Don and Herb had helped me build when Mother stopped me.

"I was glad to hear you had decided to apply to Bradley," she said.

I stared at her. "What?!"

"Well, when Pris said you could always say no if they accepted you, you said 'Sure.'"

Christ Almighty, what had I done? "I was just acknowledging the truth of her statement," I said, aware that I was talking too fast. "In principle only. I promise you, I have no plans *whatever* to leave John Dewey High. Please . . . think of chess club, the literary magazine—are you really going to make me give all that up?"

Mother sighed. "Nobody is going to make you do anything you don't want to do, Peggy. It's just—"

"—Leave it there," I begged. "I do not want to go to Bradley Academy for Girls. I will not apply unless you force me to. If you can call that 'indecision,' fine, but it's *not!*" Before she could answer (or more likely, cry), I tore out the back door and climbed up to my sanctuary. But I had an awful feeling it could offer only solitude, not safety.

Ω

The tennis court became a reality while the barn retained what the Great Man called its Platonic form. The reason, I gradually realized, was that Herb and Don needed more incentive to spend weekends in Vermont than cutting brush or weeding vegetables. Nor were they alone. As Don put it, "The whole summer crowd's looking for a place to play," and if we had a court, we'd provide a focus for those people.

The focus began before the court was even built. After Don and Herb visited the Hendersons' court, one tanned, athletic young man after another dropped by "to look at our site," and the next Saturday, an older tanned, athletic man with "Net Works Unlimited" on his truck came into the kitchen with plans and estimates and left two hours later with a check. After Herb and Don took off for a celebratory beer, I spotted the Great Man whacking a croquet ball moodily around the lawn and went out to join him.

"Is it *really* gonna happen?"

"Looks like it."

I took courage from the ambivalence in his face. "But . . . *here?* On a farm?"

He sighed. "Peggy, sometimes you have to let the younger generation lead the way. It's going to be their world, after all."

"What about the people in the younger generation who like Vermont the way it is?"

He raised his eyebrows. "You don't want a court? Last I heard, your tennis had gotten so good you could have been on the JV team if we hadn't spent summers here."

"Well, yeah. But liking tennis is different from building a court of your own."

"You think so, do you?"

I felt treacherous waters lap around my ankles. "Um . . ."

"But you do like the snappy little car, and the piano, and the barn, when we build it."

"The barn is real Vermont—horse, tractor, lumber, work-bench, tools. As for the others, you can play with those by yourself . . ."

". . .Without looking nouveau riche?"

I tried to smile as the treacherous waters reached my neck. "Well, nouveau riche is better than no riche at all."

He laughed, and I was saved—or so I thought until, after he'd trounced me in croquet, he said, "The kind of summer people the Mountain has brought here couldn't tell nouveau riche from old money if they saw the two walking down the street together."

I thought a minute. "Is that why the Hendersons don't share their court?"

He gave me one of his rare companionable smiles. "I imagine so. But though I'm guilty of the vulgarity you've so neatly identified, I haven't lost my affection for the Old Vermont. Rob Bartlett is going to be doing the initial bulldozing—"

"—Oh, keen!"

"—because Karl Zander pointed out that it might bring Rob's expertise to Mr. Net Work's attention." He smiled. "So you see, you can play tennis with your brothers-in-law and their summer crowd with the knowledge you've helped the Bartletts keep their farm. And by the way, it's going to be a very good court. You'll enjoy it."

Ω

Rob came the next day to look over the job. He was nineteen now, and he'd become as quiet as his father, so I had no idea what he thought until, after he and the Great Man had talked over the job, he turned and looked silently at the hawkweed and butter-cups that surrounded the ledge outcrop where Mr. Bartlett had taken us kids to look at the stars. Early the next morning, he and his bulldozer carved an ugly scar up the mowing for the trucks that were to follow him, and by late afternoon, he'd converted the buttercups and hawkweed into a carefully groomed pile of dirt. Mr. Net Works dropped by, admired Rob's work, and kept him on for the week it took to import innumerable truckloads of dirt and gravel. To my delight, when it came time to lay down the clay, he trained Rob to use the equipment and asked him to help with the fence. Red and I stopped by the Bartletts' to tell that to Joan, but she was working. Mrs. Bartlett told me she had a job at a Westover beauty parlor and a boyfriend and was hardly ever home. Mrs. Bartlett was leaving for work herself so she couldn't chat—and though she said I could ride through their sugar grove any time I wanted now that the cows were gone, I saw she was glad to go.

Don and Herb missed the action; they'd gone back to the city, saving their vacation time for the finished court, but Pris and Liz kept them up to date with nightly phone calls. They'd stayed around to "help poor Mother," a phrase that somehow implied I was not just unhelpful but part of the burden Mother had to bear. I consoled myself by thinking of the Third and Fairest Sister of fairy tales—Cordelia, for example—and by enjoying the two little girls, who, as the Great Man was fond of saying, were as much younger than I as I was younger than Liz and Pris. They sat spellbound when I told them stories, climbed like little squirrels into the treehouse, and "helped" me groom Red in return for riding lessons. The lessons were a source of great maternal anxiety, but after watching Red tiptoe patiently around the area I'd designated as a ring, even Mother admitted the kids were in good hands.

"Bless his heart," said Pris, patting him affectionately as she lifted Debby down. "You know, Peggy—"

"—I'm going for a ride now," I said hastily. I knew a

"sister-to-sister chat" voice when I heard one. But when she said, "This won't take long," at the same time Liz lured Debby away with promises of going to the lake, I realized I'd been out-maneuvered.

"You know, Peggy," she repeated as I walked Red towards the mounting block, "you might very well be happier at Bradley than at home."

I looked straight ahead. "Just because you were unhappy at John Dewey High doesn't mean I am. Mr. Jasper has been helping us Lit Magazine people with our writing, one of my stories got honorable mention in the Michigan Junior Writers' Contest—"

"—We heard all about that," she said. "It's great! Mother was very proud."

"So why should I give that up?"

I felt her look at me. "Because of the way things are at home."

"The only thing that's wrong at home is that they insist that Mother's trips to the hospital are just checkups." I willed away the tears that were threatening to choke my voice. "I play along with their charade because I realize that pretending everything's fine is very important to them. But since they've made you their ambassador, maybe you can *tactfully* suggest that if they *really, truly* think I don't know Mother has had three serious operations, I'm a hell of a lot better liar than they are."

"I understand," she said, in a tone that was the equivalent of Red's children's walk. "But think of how much it would help Mother to know you were all right."

"I'm perfectly all right at home! At least, I would be if you didn't all gang up to God damn *reform* me!"

"Hey, calm down," said Pris. "I'm trying to level with you."

"Level with me!" I said, vaulting onto Red's back. "Oh, sure! With a nine-foot drop." And to Red's surprise, we took off at a canter.

We went back to a walk as soon as we were out of sight of the house, but my angry thoughts roiled around me until we got near the Hapneys' and Red pricked up his ears. There was often machinery going in and out there, so I snapped to attention, but all we saw as we rounded the corner was a bay quarter horse and a rider in a cowboy hat talking to Mr. Wolfson. The talking stopped, presumably not because they'd run out of things to say but because the horse neighed and reared.

We halted, but Mr. Wolfson shouted "Hey, Peggy! C'mon by!"

I urged Red forward uneasily, knowing all too well that equine shenanigans were often contagious and that there was no guarantee I could survive them bareback. But though Red snorted a time or two, he walked on quietly as the quarter horse backed, danced, and bucked.

"Atta girl," said Mr. Wolfson. "Now, do Jake here a favor, if your hoss'll let you. Walk down to the ring there, then turn around and come back."

So that was the famous Jake, who could keep his seat on any horse Joe the Frenchman brought home. I glanced at him as we went by, and he tipped his hat, his face and seat alike undisturbed by the turmoil underneath him. Red balked as I turned him past the barn, but he went on as I insisted, turning his head only once at the explosion of hoof-beats behind us. With almost as much respect for Red as for Jake, I rode around the ring and back to the road. Apart from some dancing in place, the quarter horse was standing still.

"Thanks," said Jake. "Think your hoss has it in him to go back to the ring with us followin'?"

Mr. Wolfson frowned. "S'posin' I lead him. Then he don't have to be a saint."

But Red declared his sainthood by turning when I asked him and walking so calmly you'd never have known a horse was prancing and sidling behind him. At Mr. Wolfson's signal, Red and I walked around and around the ring with halts at both ends, watching Jake patiently turn bucking, backing, and rearing into a jittery but convincing imitation of what we were doing.

"Okay," he said finally. "Let's line up."

I halted in the center, and when Jake pulled up next to us, the horse actually stood still long enough for him to dismount. I was so awestruck that I remembered only at the last millisecond to adopt an androgynous voice and tone. "They *told* me you could ride," I said.

Mr. Wolfson laughed as Jake blushed and made himself busy with his saddle. "You ain't seen *nothin'*!" he said. "This is one of the quiet ones."

I thought he was kidding, but Jake nodded. "Treat him decent, he'd be like your hoss," he said. "He's only three, don't know shit from Shinola, and nobody ever bothered to show him the difference." He spat in disgust. "Those places out west beat 'em up, call 'em broke, and ship 'em here where prices are higher. I thought of workin' out there an' doin' it right—but I'll turn eighteen next spring, an' my last name's Abney."

I said, "Too bad," because he seemed to expect a response, but it was only after he'd started leading the horse towards the barn that I realized he had to be talking about the draft.

After he got through the gate, he turned around, "Look how quiet this guy is when nobody's on him," he said. "It's a cryin' shame. S'posin' I was to ask Joe for a week with him, and we tag along with you so he can see how a good hoss acts?"

"No go," said Mr. Wolfson quickly. "Peggy's folks don't want her dealin' with Joe—'fraid she'll get hurt. An' you gotta hand it to 'em. They found her a hoss in a million." He patted Red, looking up at me so kindly I felt bad all over again. "Say, I see you've got some excavatin' goin' on up at your place. They buildin' you a ridin' ring?"

"Don't I wish," I said. "It's a tennis court."

"Jeesum!" Jake turned and stared at me.

"Listen," I said. "Let me ask my parents if you can take a young horse out with Red and me. If they say yes, I'll tell Mr. Wolfson and he can tell you. That okay?"

"No call to make trouble," he said, pleasantly enough, but in a flat voice nobody could mistake. "Joe's in a hurry for this guy anyway." And he led his horse into the barn.

Ω

The tennis court was ready for action by mid-July. It looked raw and out of place, but nobody else seemed to care. In August, when my brothers-in-law both took vacations, every time you looked up the mowing, you could see white-clad people jumping, bending, or serving. The men all looked vaguely like Herb and Don, though some were old enough to have kids my age, and their wives, with whom Mother, Liz, and Pris chatted over post-tennis drinks, were athletic, vivacious, and hard to tell apart.

The Great Man, whose wicked chops and spins failed to compensate for feet that stayed rooted to the court, admitted to being outclassed, and opted out of playing with anybody but the family and Mr. Zander. I tried to follow his example, taking long rides that made me unavailable for most of the day, but the strategy proved impossible to sustain. Pris and Liz said "poor Mother" worried if I wasn't home in time for lunch, and although I suspected their motives—child entertainment was one of my primary domestic skills—I knew that the only thing standing between me and the Bradley Academy application blank was faultless behavior. That included being on afternoon call as a fourth in mixed doubles—and hey, Don asked sardonically, was it too much to ask me to wear shorts, not horsey jeans?

It was, but for the sake of family harmony, I changed into cut-offs whenever my presence was demanded. That quickly became every afternoon, with the result that for the first time since we'd come to Vermont, I met summer people my age. At first, dismally aware that my circles and those of my Vermont friends no longer intersected, I welcomed the prospect of companionship. But it soon became clear that summer-kid circles were to intersect mine only on the court—where, though I held my own well enough in doubles, I got shellacked if I challenged any of the guys in singles.

"Brother," I said, dropping down next to Mr. Zander, after a six-love set with a kid named Dave had prompted me to give over the court to Don. "That was humiliating."

"Actually," he said, "it was impressive. You brought every serve to a rally and brought several games to a deuce. Boy, was he surprised."

"Hrmph," I said. But as I watched him slam back Don's serve, rush the net, and put away a wicked shot to his backhand, I was a little surprised myself. "He's good."

"Good enough to be New England State champion for the last two years and captain of the Andover tennis team. I gather both Yale and Harvard are recruiting him."

I watched Dave's overshot end a ferocious rally. "Andover's a prep school, right?"

"Yep. Like the Pope's Catholic."

I could never think of the Pope's being Catholic without remembering Grammy's earnest wish that he become a good Presbyterian, but this was no time for nostalgia. "Same for Exeter and Groton and Deerfield?"

He was looking at me now. "You got it."

"It's amazing how *many* places there are to send your kids if you don't want them around."

"That's not the only reason parents send their kids to prep schools."

"Right," I said. "There's also status. The first question Dave asked me was where I went to school. And when I said John Dewey High, he and his friends kind of looked at each other and . . . well, you could see me falling off their radar screens."

"Ah," he said. "That's a pity."

"I suppose so," I said. "I wish they knew how interesting my friends at John Dewey High are. Math whizzes. Writers. Musicians. And every one of them knows the difference between capitalism and democracy."

"The ultimate IQ test," he said, laughing. "Listen, though. I know what you're hitting with these kids, but give them a little time. You're not what they're used to."

"It's no big deal." I watched Dave make an incredible return. "At least, it wouldn't be if I weren't under pressure to become one of them."

He looked at me sharply. "What's this?"

"Mother wants me to go to Bradley Academy."

"Since when?"

"Since April, I guess. That's when I took the prep school exams."

"April," he muttered. Then, getting up—"Let's take a walk."

"Sure," I said, scrambling to my feet. "I have to check Red's salt lick."

"Hey, stick around for doubles!" shouted Don.

Mr. Zander grinned. "We'll be back before he's finished with you."

We ducked under the fence that separated the mowing from the pasture and walked up the hill. Below us, the valley sloped down to the lake in fields and woods rimmed by the hill of the Bartletts' mowing and, beyond that, the mountains. I adjusted the salt lick on its ledge and focused my eyes on Red, who was slowly grazing his way towards us.

"Tell me about Bradley Academy," said Mr. Zander. "Your parents and I discussed it last August, after the 'ladies' mount' incident, but I thought I'd talked them out of it."

I fought back a tide of hope. "What on earth did you *say?*"

"Among other things, that somebody who has steadfastly refused to follow the accepted rules of femininity and who has managed to compete successfully on her own terms would not be happy at a girls' school. They saw my point so completely that I thought the subject was closed. But you say it was reopened last spring, which leads me to the forbidden subject of your mother's health." He paused. "Has she had . . . further treatment?"

"Yeah. Ten days in the hospital last September and two weeks last February."

"Dear God," he whispered. "Then it metastasized."

"It what?"

"Metastasized," he said. "It's the word for cancer that has left its initial location and spread into other parts—"

"—Cancer," I repeated. "She has cancer?"

He looked at me incredulously. "You didn't know?"

I watched Red look suspiciously for a halter and lead rope as he moved closer. "No. Just that it had to be something serious. They don't talk about it. Ever."

"I know. Your father prevaricated even when I asked him point blank. I had to worm it out of him. But it never occurred to me that *you* didn't know."

"I think Pris and Liz know. That's why they've been here so much. But I guess they think I'm too dumb to notice." I reached mechanically into my pocket as Red stopped expectantly in front of me.

"There's a difference between thinking you're too dumb to notice and wanting to protect you from the possibilities that go with metastasizing cancer."

I gave Red a tired piece of carrot. "Are you sure it's just me they want to protect?"

"As opposed to . . . ?"

"Themselves," I said. "If I don't notice, it's not happening."

"That's very perceptive," he said, "and partly true. It's not the whole story, though."

"Okay, but if she's getting worse . . . that's what you're saying, right?"

"I'm afraid it is."

"Well, then maybe the only way they can keep pretending is to send me to Bradley Academy, where I *can't* notice, so it *keeps* not happening." I watched a crow fly towards the lake. "Plus, well, I really try to cooperate, but sometimes—"

"—Peggy! You *mustn't* blame yourself. I promise you, they don't want to send you away because you're trouble."

"You sure?" I said bleakly. "I'm not what Mother wants . . . gracious, ladylike . . ."

"Nonsense! Your mother may have some Louisa May Alcott ideas about a woman's place, but she's extremely proud of you. You're much closer to the truth when you say they're trying to protect themselves. Cancer is tougher than anything they've ever encountered. They're worried about its effect on you, and they're trying to find a solution."

I glanced at him. "Does that mean you don't think you should stop them from sending me away?"

He looked out at the mountains, jingling the car keys in his pocket until he noticed it gave Red false hopes. "It means I'll have to think very carefully about how to do it. If I do it wrong, I'll be trespassing in a deeply personal area where I have no right to go."

No right to go. *You have no __right__ to make you mother clean up after you* . . . Did I have the right to make the horror of cancer worse by refusing to be sent away? Hadn't Pris sort of hinted that doing what Mother wanted was the only way I could help?

I longed to jump on Red's back and ride down, down, down the long hill to the lake, but my chances of completing a romantic, bridleless escape without falling off were nil. So I shooed him back to his grazing and turned to Mr. Zander. "Don't talk to them. I think I should go."

"Are you *sure?*"

I studied him. Behind the sadness in his face was a look that told me he was behind me all the way. And somewhere in there, along with pity, there was a little glimmer of respect.

"As sure as I'll ever be."

He had the good sense not to say anything. We just stood there, looking out at the view, until finally I made myself smile at him. "We'd better get back to the court," I said. "It's time we preppies took on you old folks."

Daedalus and Perdix

From my point of view, the year I turned sixteen was an unqualified success. I left John Dewey High with a triple award in citizenship, academics, and sports. Bradley Academy lay ominously on the horizon, but as summer started I faced my doom with a confidence buoyed up by my past spring's inclusion into an upperclassman circle that depended not on the frippery of dating, but on acting, painting, singing, and writing. Everything would have been perfect, except that the thrill of intellectual companionship was qualified by my knowledge that the year was a disaster for my parents. The unhappiness of Liz and Herb's marriage, disguised for Mother's benefit the previous summer by his absence in the city or on the tennis court, had escalated—despite a thousand phone calls—into the disgrace of divorce. The eagerly-planned tour of Europe had been dogged by Mother's increasing weakness and capped by a fourth long hospital stay upon their return. And as if that weren't enough, I was getting pretty.

Left to myself, I would have put prettiness on the plus side of the ledger, but comments by my parents' friends ("You'd better look out, Ned—you've got a hot item there!" or "Boy, Ellen, you're really gonna have to keep an eye on her now!") added the threat of my imminent moral lapse to the list of parental anxieties. So when Mr. Zander, coming over as usual with dinner to welcome us up for the summer, stared at me and said "Why, Peggy! You've become a beauty!" I told him in no uncertain terms that looks were *not* a subject for discussion in our family. The shock in his face as Mother appeared behind me made my point clear.

Neither unexpected beauty nor its sudden absence could faze Mr. Zander for long. He bestowed hugs all around, put a pan of lasagna in the oven, and let us walk him to the newly-completed barn, where he admired the spotless workroom, laughed at the outsized box stall that awaited my summer horse, and helped the Great Man jump start the tractor. Back in the kitchen, he served antipasto and chianti with his usual flourishes as he listened to anecdotes of their European trip. The only snag occurred when he turned to the Great Man with, "How's Ovid coming? The last thing I saw was that marvelous rendition of Icarus plunging into the sea."

The Great Man sipped his chianti, felt in his inner pocket for a cigarette, thought better of it, and said, "Icarus. Yes, yes. I'll have Perdix to show you soon."

If you didn't know your Ovid, you wouldn't think anything of it. But if you did, you knew that Ovid had placed the story of Perdix—the brilliant boy Daedalus pushed off the Acropolis out of jealousy for his skills—immediately after Icarus's famous fall, so the alert reader would understand that the fall was Daedalus's punishment for his sin. Mr. Zander's expression told me we were thinking the same unthinkable thought: in eight months, the eighty-line story of Perdix was *all* the Great Man had translated . . . ?

Rather than let the possibility waft about in the lasagna-smelling silence, I babbled, "Guess what! I'm learning to drive—in this state I'll be able to get a license in a month!"

The Great Man, who had been staring out the window, came back to life. "She's doing very well."

"Stick shift or automatic?" said Mr. Zander.

"Automatic, unfortunately," said the Great Man. "Stick

wasn't available on the Skylark."

"I can provide stick shift, if you'd like," said Mr. Zander. "Even in this technological age, every driver should know how to use a clutch."

I stared at him in disbelief. "You'd let me drive the MG?"

He laughed. "Not right away. You'd have to start on my old Ford. But if, beyond mastering the intricacies of the clutch, you can convince me you're a *real* driver . . ."

"You bet I can!" I said—and in spite of all the moral dangers prettiness had thrust upon me, I jumped up and threw my arms around his shoulders.

Ω

My horse arrived the next afternoon. There was the usual bustle of getting the trailer situated properly, lowering the ramp, and so on—so it wasn't until the horse finally backed out onto the driveway that I realized the guy holding his halter was Jake.

"Here you go," he said, handing me the lead rope.

I looked the horse over, ignoring the appraisal I sensed I was receiving. Green Mountain Stables had informed us that Red was "no longer available" and had offered a hunter in his place. The delicate bay stepping around on the lawn was no more a hunter than Red had been a Morgan, but he was handsome, and I reached out to make friends. He threw up his head and shied away.

"Some fool's twisted his ear, most likely," said Jake. "A little time, you can fix that. An' look, when you put him out to pasture, don't catch him before you ride him, see? Bring him in to feed him, an' let him wait around inside."

I nodded, gloomily comprehending his unspoken message. "Okay. I'll start him out in his stall."

"Good move," he said—and to my surprise, after checking to see that Mother was still involved with the paper work, he walked to the barn with us. "Been watchin' this go up," he said. "It's always interestin' to see 'em . . . Holy Jesus! That's a *stall*?"

I blushed as I unsnapped the lead rope. "Not the one I asked for. It was supposed to be a twelve by twelve box, but they added an outside door and nailed the interior wall to the uprights."

"It's gonna give him an outsize notion of himself," he said, grinning as the horse checked out the feed dish, snatched a bite of hay, and stuck his head out the window. "You'll have to call him Prince or somethin'."

Not Prince, I thought sadly. "How about Emperor?"

"C'mon, Emp . . . steady, Emp . . ." he said experimentally. "Sounds good to me."

Emp turned away from the window and strolled over to the door. His ears wavered forward as I reached into my pocket, and he warily let me pat him as I gave him a carrot. "What's his story—do you know?"

"All I know is, Green Mountain called Joe this mornin' sayin' they had a delivery to make but their driver was sick. So Joe sent me to do the hoss work; their guy's doin' the business." He looked back at Emp as he started towards the door. "I'd say he's from some ridin' school, gone sour from too many lessons."

I sighed. "I wish I could rent a horse without a story."

"They all got stories," he said, shrugging. "That's what makes 'em interestin'—figgerin' out their stories from the way they act." He paused in the doorway. "Y'know, I ride interestin' stories by here pretty often now that there's that new snowmobile path through Bartletts' sugarbush. Sure would help 'em to have company that acted right."

I turned in surprise—his scorn of tennis courts and his certain knowledge of the whole "ladies' mount" affair was seared into my consciousness. The guarded expression of his light blue eyes told me it wasn't all gone, either. But no question—the offer was genuine.

"Sounds *great!*" I said. "But my parents . . ."

He nodded. "Lemme see what I can do." He turned and walked down the driveway, his high-heeled boots leaving little marks in the dirt. When he got to Mother, he tipped his cowboy hat and said, "Every time I ride past, I look at your flowers an' think about my granny. She lived in this house."

"Really?" Mother's interest was immediate. "How long? When?"

"I dunno for certain," he said. "Think she moved on durin' the thirties—got foreclosed or evicted or somethin'. Story of her life. But wherever she moved to, she planted flowers."

"Would she talk to us?" said Mother. "I've begun to write a history of this house."

Jake shook his head. "She died when I was a kid. But I can ask my mom what she knows, if you'd like. She likes flowers, too. Gardens for lotsa summer folks."

Hope dawned in Mother's emaciated face. "Would she have time to work here? I've been wondering how I can *ever* keep the weeds back."

Jake glanced at the overgrown strip that followed the wall around the croquet court. "'Course I can't speak for Mom, but I know she likes this place. Last name's Abney—we're the only ones in the book. Give her a jingle."

"I'll call this evening! Thanks so much!"

"All right, then." Jake tipped his hat again, climbed into the driver's seat, and eased the trailer out into the road.

"What a nice young man!" said Mother.

I made my nod as neutral as I could. "He sure is."

Ω

I'd hoped that Mr. Zander would be a more active driving teacher than the Great Man, who tended to doze off once I'd gotten to country roads. And he was more active, but not in the way I'd expected. He drove his Ford onto the grass track that led to the tennis court, showed me the patterns of shifting, explained the principles of the clutch, let me start and stall a few times— and got out. "Drive up to the court, turn around, drive back, and pull into the driveway," he said. "And remember: the car will do exactly what you *tell* it to. If you expect it to do what you *want*, you'll turn it into an adversary. That's counter-productive, even if you win."

When my panic subsided sufficiently to let me think, I realized he'd enunciated something I sort of knew. The Great Man had occasionally gotten the tractor spectacularly stuck by ignoring its capacities. Jake, on the other hand, could ride anything with four legs because he could think like a horse. Therefore . . . I stared at the dashboard, the clutch, the accelerator. Okay, think like a car. It took a while, and it didn't help that the Great Man and Mr. Zander were watching from the Adirondack chairs. But the Ford gradually began to accept my offers of teamwork, and when we had to turn around at the tennis court, we even agreed to go backwards after a few tries. We finished with a nearly flawless drive back to the driveway and—I remembered just in time to apply the clutch and brake simultaneously—a gentle stop.

I was psyched, and I needed to be, because after they'd acknowledged my success, the two announced that the next lesson was How to Change a Tire. A bit much, I thought. Unnecessary hazing, damn them. But I put on my best androgynous face and told myself, *Think like a jack. Think like a lug wrench.* It worked, by God. The tire came off and went back on with only a few glitches, and the gentlemen, who had obviously anticipated a scene of whining and feminine pleas for help, didn't get their show.

"Good work, Peggy," said Mr. Zander after Mother's call for lunch had started the Great Man back to the house ahead of us. "You're a wonder."

The admiration in his face sent me into seventh heaven, but it was accompanied by something less familiar and more puzzling, so I just smiled and led the way in.

Ω

A couple of mornings after Mother called Jake's mom, a fifties Ford lumbered into the driveway just as I was leading Emp out of the barn. Figuring it was somebody to see the Great Man, I stuck my left foot in the stirrup, but the car's door opened with a squawk, and Emp spooked. Pulling on the reins, I hopped helplessly in his wake, unable either to swing on or to wrench loose, until an authoritative hand grabbed his bridle right under the bit. When I finally dislodged my boot, I saw that my savior was a woman with a worn face and light blue eyes that met mine with a mixture of reserve and amusement.

"Thank you," I said, shaken. "I should never have let it happen."

She shrugged. "Everybody gits caught out now'n then. You Peggy?"

"Yes," I said, searching my mind for a name to go with the face.

"Susan Abney," she said.

"Oh!" I said "Jake's mom!"—then, recovering my manners, I added, "Jake's a terrific rider. He's just *amazing.*"

"He's a good boy." She studied me with an expression I couldn't quite interpret. "I told your mom I'd stop by to see her garden. She inside?"

Just as I said yes, Mother came out the back door and waved.

"Seems everything's set," said Mrs. Abney. "Here, climb on while I'm still holdin' your hoss."

I swung on, which killed further conversation—once you were in the saddle, he expected action right away. "I'm really glad you've come," I said, trying to sit as still as Jake did. "The weeds have . . ." I broke off as Emp went into a pirouette.

"You better git goin' while he still wants to go the same way you do," said Mrs. Abney—and I took her advice, covered with shame. Jake wanted me to help his "stories" learn decent behavior, and I couldn't even mount! I cursed Emp for being skittish until he got *so* skittish that it dawned on me that my cursing was making it worse. If I thought like a school horse, I'd . . . oh, yeah . . . I'd realize he was used to a lot more work and less grain than I'd been giving him. I could almost feel him relax as the idea came to me, and three hours of trotting and cantering later, he walked the last mile in without giving stumps, mailboxes, or cows even a passing glance.

Mr. Zander's MG had replaced Mrs. Abney's car in the driveway, but my sudden flash of hope faded when I saw him talking to mother—in whites.

"Just in time, Peggy!" he called as I crossed the lawn. "Doubles in half an hour."

My aching muscles muttered that we should have trotted and cantered a bit less. "With whom?"

"Dave Robinson and his dad. Should be good tennis."

"We saved you a sandwich," said Mother. "But look at the garden!"

It looked transformed, even to my unpracticed eye. Irises bloomed alone where they'd shared the territory with goldenrod before; lupines shot up out of neatly-groomed lower leaves, and poppies blazed in a corner that had been hidden by choke cherries. "Wow!" I said. "She did all that in three hours?"

Mother nodded. "She's a dynamo." She turned to Mr. Zander. "What a godsend! And all because her son's one of Peggy's admirers."

"He's *not*—!" I began, but Mr. Zander's smile told me it was too late.

"An admirer!" he said. "Tall? Dark? Handsome?" I turned

away in disgust, but he wouldn't leave it alone. "C'mon, Peggy— what's he look like?"

I shrugged. "Like Shane."

Mother laughed. "I hadn't thought of that, but it's true. Not just the hat and boots—the self-possession."

"He comes by it honestly," I said. "He's gotta be the best rider in Southern Vermont."

"Really?" Mr. Zander's eyebrows rose.

"Really," I said. "If you watched him with a horse for five seconds, you'd see he's got the same kind of discipline and understanding as the Spanish Riding Academy guys, only of course he rides Western for Joe the Frenchman, so nobody notices. —Look, if I don't eat that sandwich, I'll collapse on the court."

I hurried inside, changed while devouring the sandwich, and got back to the yard just as Mother and Mr. Zander were greeting the Robinsons. The first thing Mr. Robinson said was that he was the father of a Harvard man now, and as he went on about the glorious achievement, Dave glanced first at me, then up at the court. I nodded, and we were on our way before the grownups realized we were gone. The escape should have produced an air of camaraderie, but the swirl of furious embarrassment behind Dave's polite façade made conversation impossible. When we got to the court, I turned to him.

"About your dad," I said unlatching the gate. "Don't sweat it. We all have families."

He stared at me, then a real smile broke through his veneer— and a moment later he paid me the compliment of pasting balls to me as hard as he could. Honed by ferocious spring practice under the eye of John Dewey High's coach, I managed to get a racket on almost everything he hit, but rally after rally ended when my returns went long or wide. Finally, out of desperation, I hexed one of his shots with a vicious chop, and watched with satisfaction as he scrambled for it and missed.

"Dirty tennis!" he said, grinning. "Where'd you pick that up?"

"From my old man," I said. "It's one of many tricks that keep me from beating him."

"You can't beat your old man?"

"Nope. He stands there, chopping and chortling. It's *infuriating.*"

He laughed. "Like you say—we all have families." He glanced down the mowing at the two men strolling our way. "Speaking of which . . . could you smile pretty and ask my dad to be your partner?"

"Wouldn't it be more fun if we took them on?"

"Hey, there's an idea!" Instantly, his social façade dropped into place, and as Mr. Zander and Mr. Robinson walked onto the court, he made the proposal so tactfully that their initial resistance melted into acquiescence. The resulting dynamics were even more interesting than I'd anticipated. The rivalry between Dave and his father went without saying, but I hadn't expected equal ferocity in Mr. Zander. We were closely matched, so it was stimulating—or would have been, if its angry undertone hadn't marred it. In the end, we split sets, 8-6, 7-9, and walked down the mowing in silent fatigue.

"Tennis for blood, right here at home," I said to Mr. Zander as they drove off. "Men are so strange. Why care about the score when the playing's that good?"

"It's not easy to watch a talented youngster vie for your place," he said. "Just ask Daedalus. —Say, did I hear you and Dave agree to practice together?"

"Yeah," I said. "Day after tomorrow. But that can change fast if it'll interfere with clutch lessons."

"No, no. That's fine. Tomorrow?"

I hesitated. I was pretty sure Jake knew I rode in the morning, but I wasn't sure when he'd turn up, or even if he would.

"Check your social schedule," he said cryptically. "I'll call after lunch, and we'll see where things are."

Ω

Over the next few days, Jake and I gradually reached an agreement of sorts: if he had a horse to ride on the trails, he'd come by our house by nine. That meant we rode together two or three mornings a week, and unless he was riding something really restive, he stopped in the driveway and chatted with Mother while I finished saddling up. She always seemed to enjoy their conversations, but one day after we'd ridden along in mostly silent companionship, he said, "Must be hard on you, having your mom so sick."

"She'd be upset if she knew you'd noticed she's sick."

"Seems nobody could look at her and *not* notice. But that's what Mom said—she's real grateful for help, but you can't even hint that she needs it."

"Your mom's very perceptive."

"Smart as a whip—but what I'm tryin' to say is, that not noticin' stuff has gotta be as hard on you as your mom bein' sick."

I shrugged. "You get so you don't notice not noticing."

"Have it your way," he said, smiling. "Say, I saw your hoss standin' real still when you mounted up today. Looks like we did a good day's work back then."

"We sure did." More accurately, *he* sure did. The day after his mom had saved me, he'd stopped by in his black-and-white Olds, with fins in back and a pair of furry dice hanging from the rear view mirror, and he'd insisted on teaching Emp to stand still. "See, probably somebody always held him in the ring while the kids got on and then slapped him on the rump so he wouldn't balk. That means he don't know he *should* stand still while someone's mountin'. So we'll have to teach him." Teaching him took three hours—and my full attention every day after that, because Emp wasn't the only one who assumed a horse moved off as the rider hit the saddle. "Do all the horses you ride for Joe stand still when you mount?"

"'Pends on where they're headed. Gymkhana riders think dancin' 'round is a sign that a hoss has git up an' go. Reinin' guys the same. I think different, but like Joe says, we're not in the hoss business to change people. But for kids' hosses and ladies' mounts—" he grinned— "we do what you an' I did for Emp. Adds fifty bucks to the price, generally."

"Do you ever get a horse you can't sell?"

"Not us. That's one thing about workin' for Joe. I've never seen him get took."

"Where would he get took?"

"Hoss auctions. There's one down in Agawam he goes to pretty regular, an' man, if you go there without you know hosses, you get took for sure. If you do know hosses, you gotta have a heart of stone, 'cause it's the end of the line for most of 'em. Makes me kinda sick, but Joe . . . well, take last time we went. There's this girl, makes me think of you, 'cept she's dressed up fine in boots and britches—anyway, she's starin' at this ol' race-hoss with his head hangin' an' his joints all swole up. Joe takes one look and says, 'Jist you wait, hon. Someday you'll git married, and then you'll *really* have somethin' to cry about.'"

"I can just *hear* him saying it!" I shook my head. "You ever think of working for somebody else—training or something?"

"Sure I do. But just now, the Army's takin' care of all my druthers. Got the call last week—I'll be gone August first."

"You've been *drafted*? You can't get out of it?"

"Not me. Getting' out is for guys whose folks can send 'em to Harvard, like the tennis player that's courtin' you."

"He's not courting me!" I said indignantly. "We hardly even talk—just rally a few times a week."

"Yeah?" He gave me a sideways look. "Whew! I was tryin' to figger out a way of telling you he was two-timin' you."

"Two timing! How on earth could you know?"

"How *couldn't* I know, with only mebbe twenty guys my age left in the valley, an' most of those in the summer set? There's a bar out by the Mountain, with pool tables an' such, an' sometimes I drop by for a beer after work. Dave's there, often as not, with a cute blond number. We shoot pool now an' then—he's good—but I got no interest in joinin' his circle, though they'd take me, no question, if I got 'em the right stuff."

The right stuff. I stared at him, fighting the Presbyterian heritage that threatened to make me look appalled. In these days of the Beats, doing drugs was pro forma at the University, but . . . "Here? In Vermont?"

"Sure, here. *'Specially* here, you might say. Any place there's rich kids that never worked a day in their lives, there's a fortune for dealers." He steadied his horse as a squirrel shot across the path. "S'prised you didn't know, mixin' with the folks you do."

It was an accusation—and not just of being naïve. But apart from arguing that I mixed with the tennis crowd only on the court, what could I say? I was rich. I'd never worked a day in my life. I was being sent to prep school, headed for college—I was like them, no matter how much I wanted to be just me.

Ahead of me, Jake turned up a steep path so small I'd never noticed it, and suddenly we were in a clearing at the top of a hill. No, not a clearing. A graveyard. I looked past the old stones at the long view over the maples, then back at Jake, whose face was so undefensive that I dared to say, "How did you find this?"

"It's easy, if you come in the front way," he said, pointing to a two-track road on the far side. "I ride up here a lot—my dad's grave is over there. The one with the little flag."

I rode along the wall. Beside the flag, a wood cross read *Jacob Abney 1925-1960.*

Emp moved uneasily as Jake's horse came closer, so I turned to face them. "I'm sorry," I said quietly. "I didn't know."

"No way you could have," he said. "And no call to be sorry. He had cancer—the doc said it prob'ly came from bein' posted in Hiroshima to clean up in '45. That was hard for Mom, but he . . . he jist chatted with us about old times, an' well, it was hard takin' care of him at the end, but the *losin'* part was okay 'cause we were all together." He looked back from the cross to me. "I wish there was some way I could tell your mom that. I hate to see her so lonesome."

I started to answer but found I couldn't. The cross blurred against the mountains and the uncertain gray-blue of the lake.

Beside me, Jake's horse jittered and half reared. He stroked its neck and turned towards the two-track road. "Time to move on," he said.

Ω

I got my driver's license the day after my sixteenth birthday. The road test was a breeze after Mr. Zander's lessons, which had included parallel parking the Ford on a steep hill, backing it through a maze of cones, and driving it frontwards between a sawhorse Scylla and Charybdis with three inches on each side. I drove home with nascent visions of freedom—until the Great Man nixed them by informing me that I could do no solo driving until I'd clocked up five hundred miles with a licensed driver in the car.

"Does it matter *what* licensed driver is in the car?"

"Not so long as he's over twenty-five."

That made the issue clear enough. When the Great Man became absolutist—and to give him credit, he rarely did—pleading only made him dig his heels in. I drove on, resolving to think like a parent. "I take it this was the rule for Liz and Pris, too?"

"It was slightly different. We insisted they drive five hundred miles *before* they got their licenses. But you've barely put two hundred on this car."

"I've put a lot of miles on Mr. Zander's Ford."

He nodded reluctantly. "The point is to keep your mother from worrying about your level of experience."

Quick thinking saved me from snapping, "Define 'experience!'"

He pulled a cigarette from the pack in his pocket and looked at it thoughtfully. "Actually, you already drive better than Liz and Pris."

"Thanks," I said, with as little irony as I could manage.

When we got home, the MG was standing in our driveway. The Great Man told me to let him out and put the Skylark in the barn. Ever obedient but still seething at parental inconsistency, I walked back—and met Mr. Zander, who gave me a congratulatory hug.

"Great work, Peggy!" he said. "Your old man said you did yourself proud."

"Thanks. Did he also say—?"

"—Never mind what he said. Remember when I told you when you became a *real* driver, you could learn to drive the MG?"

"Oh!" I stared at him, comprehension slowly dawning.

"It's not a piece of cake," he said sagely. "Even after you learn to manage four on the floor, it will take you five hundred miles to really get the hang of sports car driving. But if we clock up, say, fifty miles a day, you'll be an expert in just a bit over a week."

I thought of cursing male collusion for the way it condescended even as it proffered solutions. But then I thought again and said that would be great.

And it was.

True to form, Mr. Zander didn't let me leave the driveway until I could shift into any gear he asked without looking down. Even so, I spun out the first time we started and stalled the second. Soon, though, we were off, and within minutes I'd discovered an MG was to a Skylark as an Arabian was to a Percheron. Instant response. Beautiful control in each gear. No swaying on curves. A living accelerator under the right foot. The first two fifty-mile journeys whizzed past with me absorbed in the glories of the experience, and Mr. Zander silently smiling and offering occasional tips.

The third day it poured. I assumed that meant there would be no drive, but at the appointed hour, the MG pulled into the driveway with its top up.

"Time to learn to learn dirty-weather driving," said Mr. Zander as I hurried outside.

Dirty-weather driving turned out to be oddly unfamiliar, but more for the unexpected intimacy than the slippery surface. The roof magnified Mr. Zander's presence even as it shut out the trees and sky, and when I asked, "Where are we going?" I was suddenly aware that I could talk without raising my voice.

"Wardsboro," he said. "You can practice negotiating the curves going down the mountain without hitting the brakes any more than necessary."

As we drove towards Wardsboro through Westover, I looked at the growing strip of condominiums, ski rental places, and Swiss-imitation lodges with more than passing interest. "Is there a place here that has pool tables?" I asked, trying to sound casual.

"Sure. Andy's Bar and Grill—coming up on our right."

It looked sleazy, but there were quite a few cars in front of it. Including the blue Mercedes I'd come to associate with Dave.

"D'you ever go there?"

"Not as much as I used to. There're still some locals, but the atmosphere has changed."

"Right. The college crowd."

I felt him look at me. "You don't mix with them, do you?"

"When have I mixed with anybody up here?"

"Okay, okay. I just happen to know that they're involved with—"

"—Of course they are," I said, delighting in my worldly wisdom. "Don't worry. Grammy taught me all about the wages of sin."

"It's not sin I worry about," he said. "It's scrambling your intellectuals. There's stuff out there that does a permanent job. I've lost two students that way."

"You won't lose me," I said, smiling. "Promise."

"That's good to hear."

I ignored whatever it was in his voice that made me uneasy. "They're bored. All Dave can talk about is never spending another summer here."

"Rural Vermont loses its luster when you're eighteen or so. You'll see."

"Dave doesn't know rural Vermont exists! He lives in the Mountain's plastic bubble."

"Watch it, Peggy—brake *now*, before the curve. Good. But see where it drops off up there? You'll want to downshift into third."

The downshift was a bit louder than it should have been, but we went around the curve at a respectable pace with no brakes.

"Good," he said. "Now back into fourth until two hundred yards before the next drop. —I thought you *liked* Dave."

"He's really improved my tennis," I began . . . and suddenly I saw. "For Pete's sake. Is it worry about *him* that's behind the five hundred mile rule?"

"Well," he said evasively, "when a quintessentially eligible young man plays solo tennis with a pretty girl several times a week, you might very well suspect . . ."

I downshifted with a roar. "So you're in on it!"

"Don't take it out on the car, Peggy."

"Sorry." I negotiated the curve, only slightly chastened.

"And since you asked—I'm in on it to *circumnavigate* the five hundred mile rule."

That didn't quite ring true. "But you're concerned about Dave—and Jake, too, I bet."

He sighed. "When you get to be my age, you know how easy it is to make a choice that ruins the rest of your life."

"If they—if you—are worried that Jake will persuade me to make a choice that will land me in rural Vermont for the rest of my life, you're condemning yourself, not him! Damn it, Jake Abney wouldn't touch me with a ten-foot pole! It's my good luck he has the grace to transcend what I am and go riding with me! And as for ruining life, what about the *absence* of choice? Jake goes into the army next week. Anybody who's worried about a nonexistent romance could have found that out by *asking*, but no, no, you protect a pretty girl by creating a fantasy about her future—and then making sure she adheres to your plot!"

"Peggy—brake *now!*"

I feathered the brakes hard, downshifted and took the S-curve faster than I would have liked. I expected a reproof, but instead he said, "Jake's been *drafted?* For Christ's sake, hasn't anybody counseled him?"

"Who'd do that? Joe the Frenchman? Mr. Wolfson? Mr. Weller? They all assume serving your time is something a man does. I did ask the Great Man if there was anything we could do, but he said the army would be a good choice for Jake—he'll get out of Vermont, see new places, maybe learn some skills."

"With all due respect to your father," he said, with bitterness that surprised me, "those old saws have been outmoded for years. Didn't he even tell Jake that if he enlisted in the Navy or the Air Force, he'd be less likely to be sent to our latest imperial venture?"

"He's never talked to Jake. And what imperial venture are you talking about?"

"Read the news, Peggy! The domino theory has led this benighted country to 'contain communism' in Vietnam. It may come to nothing, but at present it means Kennedy's tripled our troop level there twice in the last two years." He shook his head. "Rob Bartlett didn't get involved in all that because I helped him show the army he was essential to his family's support. Isn't Jake's mom a widow?"

"Yeah. His father died of cancer from serving in the Hiroshima cleanup."

"Oh, Peggy," he said, and there was no mistaking the distress in his voice. "Why didn't you *tell* me?"

"Because of the way you played tennis against Dave and teased me about Jake. It stood to reason . . . I mean, we've been friends for years and years, and I figured you felt bad about not having me all to yourself."

I'd just wanted to defend myself for not having asked his advice. It wasn't until I looked sideways and saw his stricken face that I realized what I'd done.

Ω

The day before Jake left Vermont, he came by on the best horse he'd ridden all summer—a bay mare with a face that had quality written all over it. I thought we'd probably ride up to the graveyard, but he didn't want to. "Too many goodbyes already," he said. "Includin' a send-off at Joe's tonight—no ladies present." He shook his head. "Not my style, but what can you do? He got me a start, treated me right."

"He better have! Look how many horses you've helped him sell! What'll he do without you?"

"He'll figger somethin' out. Already has, for that matter. Coupl'a guys from Agawam came up yesterday, rode a few hosses."

"Were they any good?"

"Middlin'. One of 'em had real trouble with the hoss I'm

on now. Took him a quarter hour to figger out she needs a light touch."

"No kidding? *I* can see she needs a light touch."

"Yeah," he said. "But you're more'n middlin'."

He took off at a lope before I could thank him—and for the rest of the ride, he hardly talked at all, which was fine with me. The rainy day in the MG had taught me the dangers of saying what I felt.

When we got back to our barn, Pris and Don had just arrived, and as soon as Debby saw me, she ran towards us, squealing with delight. Emp just pricked up his ears, but Jake's mare reared so high I could see even he was worried she'd go over backwards.

"Gotta wonder what her story is," he said, bringing her down quietly. "A cryin' shame. I'd best be goin'—take care."

"You, too," I said. "Will you be back?"

"Not sure. Mom can't make it without my paycheck, so she's goin' to her sister's place in Montana. Good hoss country." He tipped his hat and rode away—not a moment too soon, either, because Debby, who had been transfixed with admiration when his horse reared, had carefully walked towards me and was giving me a hug.

"Who was the cowboy, Peggy? Where's Red? Can I ride this horse? Hey—are you okay, Peggy?"

"Sure I am," I said, picking her up while Emp looked on tolerantly. "Why wouldn't I be?"

Femininity Quotients

Latin grace, sung in unison by two hundred forty voices, mingled in the air with the odor of onions, cabbage, and mashed potatoes. The singers stood behind their chairs in groups of ten around white-clothed tables, wearing dresses that fell two inches below their knees, seamless stockings, and high heels. As grace concluded, each senior seated the teacher at the head of her table, then walked to the foot, a signal that the rest could sit. Quiet chatter broke out as one girl from each table fetched a tray of food from the kitchen.

It was my turn to fetch, and although I was in my second Bradley semester and knew the drill, the prospect of carrying a tray while wearing heels still made me vaguely anxious. Giving way to the pushier girls as the kitchen door closed behind us, I dropped back in the line and smiled at Mr. O'Brian as he distributed bowls and platters.

"This looks wonderful!"

"That's me good girl," he said, smiling back.

I extended my tray. "Are you taking your grandchildren skating again this weekend?"

"I surely am."

"Lucky them! How old are—?"

"—Peggy!" hissed the girl behind me, "get *moving!*"

"Sorry," I mumbled, and teetered carefully out, wishing

I hadn't apologized. Talking to the staff wasn't one of those things that got you a demerit, like wearing jeans. But a lot of the girls seemed to think it was beneath them, and nobody official seemed to care.

Dinner passed as quickly as ceremony permitted, and at its end, the headmistress's silvery bell freed each senior to walk her teacher to the Reception Room, where the faculty gathered for coffee. While they smoked and chatted, we had a few minutes of unstructured time before Evening Study, a freedom I treasured because it enabled me to read in the absence of my roommate's incessant conversation. I started for my room, but as I passed the group that was clustered around Judy Michelson, she stopped me.

"Look!" she said, extending a snapshot of a guy in uniform. "Isn't he gorgeous?"

Like all the faces that got passed around for approval, this one was more like Dave's than Jake's, but if that didn't bother you, there was no questioning the looks. "He sure is."

"He's promised to take a leave for the *prom!*" she said. "Talk about cool! A West Point cadet!" She snapped a salute, giggling. "Oh, and Peggy, he and the guys sent us a Femininity Quotient test—want to take it?"

"Actually, I—"

"—Aw, come on," she said, and since the others joined her, I shrugged. "Sure."

"Okay. The first test is to walk down the hall, but we already watched you, so that's done. Second, suppose you've stepped on a piece of gum. Show us how you'd check your shoe."

Mentally cursing my heels and full skirt, I put my right hand on the wall, swung my right shoe to the center, held it with my left hand, and peered at its sole. To my surprise, they all giggled, but Judy shushed them.

"Fine. Now show us how you'd strike a match if it didn't get us all expelled."

I smiled. The Great Man had taught me the proper way to light a match when I was four. I held an imaginary book of matches in my right hand, put my left first finger on the head of an imaginary match, and struck inward, moving my finger at the last moment.

"Okay," said Judy, glancing at the tittering girls, "and last, show us how you carry your binder and books."

I held up both hands to my shoulder, miming carrying the green book-bag I'd imported from John Dewey High.

The giggling turned into laughter, and Judy shook her head. "Amazing!" she said. "Your femininity quotient is zero!"

I pretended to laugh along with them. "That means I failed?"

"Well," she said judiciously, "it's more a test of where you are than one you pass or fail. But *feminine* girls walk from the hips down instead of striding along, and they check the soles of their shoes by looking at them over their shoulders—only guys check them from the front. And *feminine* girls strike a match by brushing it *away* from them, not towards, like guys. And as for books, *feminine* girls carry them across their chests, like this." She demonstrated.

"Or better yet," I said, smiling, "they hand them to their boyfriends and say, 'Oh, Joe, these are so heavy! Could you please carry them for me?'"

They laughed at that, but as I turned to go, Judy caught my arm, her pretty face semi-serious. "Honestly, Peggy, you'd better watch it. If you don't do something about your femininity quotient, you'll end up like *them.*" She pointed towards the Reception Room.

I'd been going to mention Tiresias, but her warning stopped me cold. Despite their emphasis on genteel behavior, *they*—the women who ran Bradley Academy—were collectively intelligent rather than attractive. As if to illustrate the point, they began to emerge from the Reception Room in a procession of rounded shoulders, shapeless figures, sagging hems, and pinched faces.

"See what I mean?" whispered Judy as the bell sent us hurrying upstairs.

"Sure do," I whispered back.

"So be warned," she said. "Remember, they used to be girls like us."

Ω

The next morning, my roommate was in such a state about the way her hair looked that I left for chapel before the bell. As I passed the communal phone, the girl using it waved at me. "Peggy, you have a call on 2 West. Hurry—it's almost eight o'clock."

"Must be a mistake," I said. I hadn't received a phone call since coming to Bradley, and even if this one was real, it would be cut off the minute the bell rang. I went to chapel and sat in the sun that warmed my assigned place, enjoying the rare solitude and thinking of Grammy.

My first class was English 11, where ten of us obediently took notes as Miss Barnwell analyzed Gray's Elegy symbol by symbol and metaphor by metaphor. With its grandeur chopped into pieces and run through a critical meat-grinder, the poem became unrecognizable as the one the Great Man recited so movingly, and my feeling of sacrilege was so strong that I was in mortal danger of speaking up—but fortunately, the dean appeared in the door.

She raised a deprecating hand as we girls stood in her presence. "Excuse me, Miss Barnwell," she said. "I need to take Peggy Hamilton from class."

I started towards her, but she shook her head. "You'd better bring your things."

Good God. What had I done? I slid my books into my book bag, grabbed my coat, and walked past my wondering classmates.

The dean's Femininity Quotient was negative five. She walked from her shoulders down, wore thick glasses and dowdy clothes, arranged her gray hair in an unattractive bob, and carried her papers in a leather briefcase with straps. God knew how she looked at the soles of her shoes. Still, when I'd been sent to her office for anti-authoritarian behavior, she had listened attentively as I explained that I'd been . . . well, disappointed . . . to be told that Bradley's literary magazine had been discontinued because "nobody my age wrote anything worth reading." When I'd finished, she'd remarked that Miss Barnwell had a long and distinguished history of preparing Bradley girls for college work, including a record number of students who'd gotten 5s on the English Advanced Placement Exam. And incidentally, she (the dean) had found the story I'd turned in with my application very much worth reading.

Remembering my gratitude on that day, I dared to the break the uncomfortable silence between us. "May I ask what's wrong?"

She looked at me awkwardly. "It's your mother."

"Oh," I said. "She must be in the hospital again. It happens a lot."

She opened the door to her office, gestured silently towards a chair, and dialed the phone. "Professor Hamilton? Yes. She's right here. I'll put her on . . . what's that? No. No, I didn't." She handed me the receiver. "It's your father."

"Hi, Great Man," I said taking it. "What's up?"

"Well," he said. "Your mother . . . went back to the hospital two days ago." His voice was almost unrecognizable. "Perhaps you knew."

"No, I didn't. Is she okay?"

"She died last night."

I stared unbelievingly out the window.

On the other end of the phone, I heard a deep breath. "You'll want to come home for the funeral."

"Yes," I said—then looked at the dean. "That is, if it's all right—"

"Of course it is!" she said. "We'll make all the arrangements and get you to the airport by early afternoon."

I spoke into the phone. "Did you hear that?"

"Yes." Another pause. "Somebody will meet you."

"Okay." I wondered who it would be. Not Mother, obviously. She wouldn't be there, wouldn't ever . . . wasn't . . . "Oh, *Daddy!*"

The dean put her arm around me.

"Somebody will meet you," he repeated woodenly. "Tell the school to call with your flight number."

"Sure," I said.

The phone clicked as he hung up.

Ω

For some reason, the whole week I was home, Femininity Quotients niggled at the back of my mind. I caught myself watching the way my aunt carried the big family Bible when she talked to the pastor of Grammy's church about the service. When the Monday Club ladies helped Pris, Liz, and me plan the reception, I covertly studied the way they walked. When a Classics wife looked over her shoulder to check her shoe after she'd stepped on a jelly bean Karen and Debby had spilled, I almost asked her to do it again.

It was disgraceful to be thinking about that instead of grieving like everybody else, but the closer we came to the funeral, the more my mind slipped away from me and stood to one side, so absorbed in observation that I wouldn't have been surprised to catch it taking notes. It observed hemlines, for example: Shirley's skirts (as she demonstrated) just grazed the floor when she knelt down. Every time I looked in a mirror, it observed that my shoulders were sagging and my face looked pinched. Worst, it observed how lost I was in conversations with my literary magazine friends when they came to the house in a group to say how sorry they were. They'd all been passing around a book by Jack Kerouac, and of course they were arguing about it. Some of them laughed it off, teasing the more serious ones who had taken up black turtlenecks and leotards—but all of them talked about "digging" things that were "far out," mentioned visiting University students in their "pads," and heaped scorn on "squares" who were—so far as I could gather without a translator—the products of a capitalist system "slated for crashville." The politics was just Mr. Zander without the intellect, but there was no resisting the wonderful slang or the feeling that there was something really new in the midst of their irreverence. And there I stood, unfashionable, slumping, square . . . one of *Them*.

As I lay in bed the night before the funeral, watching my mind spin like a mouse in an exercise wheel, I suddenly had a revelation. I'd gone to Bradley to help my parents hide the truth of Mother's cancer. But now everybody knew the truth. So why should I go back? The Great Man needed support, and even though it wasn't my support he needed, I could at least keep him company. And in school, it wouldn't take long to rejoin my friends. I could read that book in a trice, and by the end of the semester everything would be just the way it had been.

The idea had everything going for it: logic, compassion, educational advantage, substantial financial savings. I stared into the familiar darkness, savoring it. And suddenly I realized what made the darkness so familiar: the sound of the Great Man's typewriter.

Maybe now was the time.

I got up, slid on my old ratty bathrobe, and tiptoed into the hall. The typewriter had gone quiet, and the light was on in their . . . in his . . . bedroom. Slowly, in case he should be undressing, I peeked in. The bed was turned down, and somebody had laid out his nightshirt. But except for the annotated *Vermont Life* calendar on Mother's desk, the page scrolled into her typewriter, the book she'd been going to come back to, and the vague scent of Yardley Lavender, the room was empty.

Next door, the typewriter started up again. I padded down the corridor, knocked, and opened the door a crack.

"May I come in?"

His face as he looked up was entirely familiar—intelligent, abstracted, smoking. He was wearing the same suit and tie he'd worn the day before, but that wasn't unusual; generally he changed only when Mother put something else out for him to wear.

"Time for bed, eh?"

"Not necessarily" I said. "Is this still Ovid?"

He nodded. "Orpheus."

My breath caught in my throat, but I managed to say, "Oh— then you've made lots of progress!"

"Not all that much," he admitted. "I skipped to it." After a pause, he added, "Even Ovid has plains between the pinnacles."

"But if you translate the pinnacles first, you'll be stuck with all those plains when you come to the end."

He came as near to smiling as I'd seen him since I'd arrived. "That's a good point. —Say, what time is it, anyway?"

I glanced at my watch. "A bit after three."

"Too bad." He glanced regretfully at the typewriter. "This passage is Ovid's greatest challenge to the translator, and I was just beginning to feel I was catching it."

And if he stopped, he'd have to face the empty room next door. "So go on with it," I said. "If you get tired, you can always take a quick nap on your sofa. Here." I gathered the books that covered it and placed them carefully on the floor.

He brightened. "That's an idea. I'll go on, then—unless there's something on your mind."

I drew a deep breath. "Well," I said, "I was just thinking that it's nice to chat about Ovid and things. Which I can't do if I'm not here. So suppose I just . . . stayed?"

"Stayed?" He looked at me blankly.

"Stayed in Michigan, I mean. With you. Transferred back to John Dewey High."

All the familiarity drained out of his face, leaving it exhausted, bewildered, lost in alien territory without a guide. "No, no," he muttered. "You go to Bradley now. That's all been settled."

I looked past him at the streetlight outside the darkened window. Of course. If I hadn't been so wrapped up in my trivial observations, I'd have known better than to ask him to deal with the world that had crashed around him.

"Don't worry about it," I said. "It was just an idea. Goodnight."

$$\Omega$$

Morning eventually came, and with it came hope. It occurred to me that if I could convince somebody else to take care of the immense mess of swapping schools, the Great Man would probably allow it to happen, if only by default. Mr. Zander would have been the perfect person for the job, but he was in Vienna on a Fulbright, and since my plane was leaving three hours after the funeral, the matter had to be settled immediately. So as the family gathered around the dining room table and the croissants the Book Club had provided, I explained the Great Man's absence by mentioning that he was asleep in his study, having worked most of the night. As I'd expected, the general head-shaking gave me a chance to say, "I'm really worried about what's going to happen to him when everybody leaves."

One of the aunts looked at me reassuringly. "A lot of their friends have promised to look in on him."

"Sure," I said. "But wouldn't it be better if I came back to school here and took care of him?"

Pris and Liz exchanged glances, and Liz muttered something about self-sacrifice.

"Self-sacrifice, phooey! Bradley's nowhere near as interesting as—"

"—Nice try," said Liz. "But we all know you're really happy at Bradley."

"How *can* you know? It's not like I showered you with letters."

"But another person in the family did," she said. "Almost every day when you were home for Christmas vacation. 'Peggy's all excited about her English class.' Or, 'Peggy let drop the news that she's captain of the varsity soccer team.'"

"'Peggy's having a great time at the glee club dances—who would have thought it?'" an uncle chimed in.

"'Peggy doesn't miss her friends at home anymore—she's become buddies with a lovely, creative girl named Judy,'" said an aunt.

I looked around the table, speechless. They were quoting the tidbits I'd offered Mother about my life at Bradley, worked casually into conversations to make them more believable. At the time they hadn't seemed mendacious—just little inventions aimed at giving Mother one less thing to worry about. I'd never dreamed that she would pass them on. "I . . . I think there might have been some . . . embellishment," I stammered. "It was very important for her to think I was happy—"

"—and very good of you to make sure she knew you were," said an uncle. "She always worried about your tomboy ways. She was just delighted to see you'd changed."

God in heaven. What could I . . .

"So of course you'll stay at Bradley," concluded the aunt. "Your father will be fine. He's booked for suppers with friends every night for the next month."

Karen's milk glass teetered on the edge of the table, and Liz leaped forward to save it. As if it were a kind of signal, everybody got up and hurried off to pack, or dress, or prepare things. Only Pris stayed behind.

"Hey," she said, "I know you're worried about Daddy. So am I, frankly. He has no idea how to cope with life without Mother. You'll need help coping, yourself, and you'll get it at Bradley. Besides, you'll find it easier to adjust in a different world instead of living with all the memories here." She stacked a few plates. "But tell me. Those things you told Mother at Christmas. Were they true?"

I nearly dropped the coffee cups I'd been gathering. "I . . . well . . . I *am* captain of the soccer team. Or at least I will be, next fall."

"Ah. And the other details—the dances, the wonderful English teacher, the friends—were they, in your deathless phrase, embellishments?"

"Um . . . okay. Yeah. They were."

"So I suspected. The transformation seemed awfully sudden, but Mother believed every word. Bless you—when it comes to lying convincingly, you're right up there with Jane Austen."

"Thanks," I said bitterly. "That's comforting to know, since I've lied my way out of being able to come home."

"You've done nothing of the kind! Nobody would consent to your coming back here, even if Bradley were keeping you on bread and water."

"But—"

"No buts about it! Coming back here would mean you'd be doing the cooking, shopping, and managing—in short, being Mother to Daddy. *While* going to school. That's impossible without help, and he—" she pointed to the stairs—"isn't going to be any. Mother knew that. We *all* knew that." She patted my shoulder. "And it's not as if you'll be deserting him. You'll have all summer in Vermont."

Vermont. I hadn't even thought about Vermont. Somebody was going to have to run the Vermont household, and Pris was right—the Great Man didn't know how. He could cook, and he did dishes sometimes, but that was different from being responsible for things. As for this house . . . I looked around at the empty flower boxes, the dishes on the table, the living room cluttered with newspapers and cigarette butts, the coats on the hall sofa. Even with all these extra people around, you could see the place needed a Central Responsible Woman.

"Okay," I said shakily. "I get it."

"I thought you would. Look, I realize you wouldn't have had to lie about being happy at Bradley if the truth would have done the job. And all I have to do is look at your hip intellectual friends here to see what a shock Bradley's cloistered atmosphere must be to you after John Dewey High. Still, it's a long way from bread and water. Bradley's teachers are excellent."

"But they're all so . . . scary."

"Scary!?"

"They don't have families! They don't have lives! They aren't—"

"—faculty wives? No, bluestockings are a different type altogether. But I'd think you'd like that! You've always wanted to be somebody who *did* something with her life."

"Yeah, but not like *that*! Homely, awkward . . . heck, even girls with decent Femininity Quotients are terrified of ending up like them!"

"Girls with *what*?"

Shoot. I hadn't meant to let that slip. "Femininity Quotients. It's how you walk—"

"—You bet." She smiled as Liz opened the kitchen door. "Hey, remember Femininity Quotients?"

"For Pete's sake!" said Liz, laughing. "Don't tell me they're still around!"

I looked from one to the other. "I thought West Point guys made them up."

"They probably did—fifty years ago, and inflicted on girls

ever since. Is it the same questions? The walk, the gum on the shoe, the match, the books?"

"Yeah."

"And you thought it was *real*?"

"I . . . well, I knew it was dumb, but it's no dumber than losing at chess, or wearing your skirt two inches below the knee, or being the only one responsible for running a household, or the other rules you have to follow to be the right sort of woman. When all the rules are crazy, how are you supposed to choose between them?"

They both opened their mouths to answer—but a crash from the kitchen sent us all flying out of the dining room. By the time we'd cleaned up the plate Debby had accidentally smashed against the tap, and patched up the fingers Karen had cut as she tried to fish it out of the dishpan, it was time to get dressed for the funeral.

$$\Omega$$

The dean was the Bradley person who met me at the airport. I was surprised, and even more surprised to find I was glad to see her. She didn't say much beyond "hello," but she led the way through all the people who were rushing up and down escalators, looking for exits, and hailing taxis as if she knew right where she was going, and people moved aside and let us through. She didn't say much when we got to the car, either, because of rush-hour traffic, but when the honking and start-stopping finally thinned out, she said, "How did it go?"

"Fine," I said. Then, having learned that people talked about a funeral like a performance, I added, "The service was lovely. The music was all her favorite pieces. There were three hundred people in the church, and a big reception at our house. It was still going on when I had to leave."

In the little silence that followed, I wondered who was going to clean everything up.

She glanced at me. "How's your father?"

"He's okay, so long as he's in his study."

"Sounds like my father when my mother died—except it was his barn, not his study."

"Your father was a farmer?"

"In a small way. Twenty cows, hay, garden, at a time that was a living if you worked hard enough, and if there were two of you. Very difficult without a woman's help, though."

"But you left?"

She nodded. "I offered to stay home, but I'd gotten a scholarship to college—just about unheard of in rural Illinois back then—and he wouldn't hear of my giving it up. Turned out to be a good thing, too. He could never have found work when the farm went under—he could barely read—but we were all right because I had a job."

"At Bradley?"

"That's right."

"Is your father still alive?"

"He died shortly after the Second War." She dimmed the lights as it started to snow. "We're going to get in just in time."

I watched the flakes dance around, then become heavier. "I'm sorry you had to come all this way," I said after a while.

"Don't be. I had lunch with old friends in Cambridge. Keeps me up with the changes in the world." She slowed down without using the brakes and turned into an exit I could barely see. "We're almost there, so down to business. A few days ago, Emily moved out of your double into a triple with Judy Michelson and her roommate. They're all very happy about the change."

"So I have a new roommate?" I said, trying to sound friendly.

"No. Your room's a bit small for two, and I thought that, things being the way they are, you'd like to have your own pad."

"I beg your pardon?"

"In less hip terminology, a single."

"Sure, sure," I said, blushing. "I just didn't expect you to . . . I mean, thank you! That's far out!"

She chuckled as she drove through the Bradley gates; before us, the snow drifted through the lights from a hundred windows. "Now, about your classes."

I sighed. "I'm way behind. I took books, but the atmosphere was all wrong."

"I'm sure it was. Everybody has arranged conferences to get you caught up, except in English 11, where it won't be necessary. Miss Nelson's section is two weeks behind Miss Barnwell's; she lingers over Shakespeare instead of Hardy. They've just started on Gray's Elegy."

Her voice told me there was something I was supposed to catch and didn't. Boy, it was just amazing how tired I was. She shut off the engine, but she didn't get out of the car. "You know," she said, "I've always thought it's a shame that Gray should have been turned into fodder for Advanced Placement exams. I'm very fond of the Elegy. My parents are buried in one of those little graveyards you see here and there in the country."

My mind flew through the snow to summer, the top of a Vermont hill, and Jake, sitting quietly on his horse and looking at his father's grave. I'd wanted something like that for Mother, but my uncles and the Great Man had insisted on burying her in the Cincinnati family plot, along with Grammy, Grandfather, and the other children they'd lost in a life that had nothing to do with me. If it wasn't snowing there, they'd be on their way now . . .

"Excuse me?" I said, dimly aware that she'd said something.

"I said, usually an exchange like that's not possible, but Miss Barnwell reminded me that both English 11s meet at the same time this year."

I stared at her half-lit profile. "You mean I'm going to switch out of Miss Barnwell's section into Miss Nelson's?"

"That's right." She opened her door, letting in a knife of cold air. "You'll report to Room 332 after chapel tomorrow morning. I'll let Miss Nelson take care of the rest. —Now, let's get your suitcase out of the trunk so you can arrange your pad to your liking and get some sleep."

I hefted the suitcase through the heavy front door as she held it open, and it wasn't until it locked shut behind me that I realized she hadn't followed me. I stared at it, somehow expecting her, but then I heard an engine start up. Quickly, I fiddled with the lock, shoved the door open and, still holding it, called "Thank you!" But her lights were already moving around the circle to the road, and I wasn't sure she'd heard me.

Ω

Evening Study was still going on, so the corridor was empty as I walked to my room in the light that came from underneath a succession of doors. My own door was dark. I opened it and stood still, looking. Outside, the snow was swirling and diving in the bright row of campus lights; inside, it was bright enough to see the spaces where Emily's bed, desk, and bureau had been. My own pad. And since it was my own, I didn't have to turn on the light. I could leave my suitcase in the closet and think where I wanted things. The bed was fine, in the alcove made by the closet. But the desk . . . I kicked off the heels I'd worn ever since the funeral, rolled down my stockings, and quietly got to work.

In two minutes, I had the desk where it belonged, under the window, and the bureau on the far wall. That left room for a chair, if I could find one. Maybe I'd ask one of the maintenance men. And tomorrow, I'd think of what to put on the walls. Wasn't there a rolled up picture in my desk . . .?

As I looked, I realized that the lump I'd ignored when I'd

slid the desk to the side was a sandwich, carefully wrapped in wax paper. I sniffed. Ham and cheese with mustard. I unfolded the packaging, picked up a neatly-sliced half—and caught a little piece of paper as it fell out. Opening my hand, I saw it was a shamrock. I smiled at it. Tomorrow, I'd go to breakfast early and thank Mr. O'Brian.

The bell went off. Lights blazed in the corridor, doors slammed, and within seconds, Bob Dylan's flat voice was serenading us from the record player we all shared. ". . . And the times, they are a changin'."

Not here, they weren't. I looked out the window, munching meditatively. Everything I'd noticed at home had showed me how behind the times Bradley was—the same school, with the same teachers and the same rules Pris had over ten years ago. The fifties! Elvis! Good God.

Still, it's a long way from bread and water. I smiled at my almost-finished sandwich. That, at least, was true.

Suddenly I wanted to call Mother and tell her I'd gotten back all right, that I had a single room, that the dean didn't look the way a woman was supposed to look, but it didn't matter because she'd made herself what she'd become, which meant she could look anybody in the eye . . .

But of course I couldn't. There was no Mother to call. There was just me. Banished to Bradley for the next three semesters, with summers off to be Mother to my father. No embellishments. Well, if the dean could do it, so could I.

I turned on the light, opened the door, and stepped out into the corridor.

Gift Horse

The late-afternoon Vermont sun turned the Bartletts' mowing luminescent green as I slipped out of the Skylark, still in my graduation dress and high heels. From somewhere deep in the woods, the song of a hermit thrush celebrated the silence. Breathing in the glories around me, I accepted the burdens of the coming summer with less reluctance than I'd anticipated. That was something of a relief, because all spring I'd been disturbed by heretical desires to spend the summer somewhere—anywhere—else.

Behind me, the Skylark's trunk popped open and the Great Man lifted out my suitcases. "Hey, thanks!" I said, turning. "I'll get the other stuff and put the car in the barn, okay?"

He smiled absently, but carried the suitcases towards the house without answering, which didn't surprise me—he hadn't spoken during the whole of the three-hour drive from Bradley. I sighed, knowing he'd go to his study after he'd taken the suitcases to my room, and that would be the last I'd see of him until I made dinner and we ate it in silence (unless I talked), did dishes, and played a wordless game of chess. I'd more or less gotten used to that silence last summer, but I'd hoped it was a temporary reaction to Mother's absence. Apparently not, which meant another summer with nobody to talk to. Not to mention another summer of being the Woman Responsible for Everything.

I looked out at the view again, and it reproached me for ingratitude. The Great Man might not talk much, but he'd given me a brand new VW Bug for graduation, and a new refrigerator to replace the failing old one in the kitchen. As I'd pointed out to Pris when she'd visited last summer and suggested I needed parental support, he had his own way of being supportive—you just had to understand how he worked. She'd scoffed. ("When has he *ever* been supportive? How would he have learned, when Mother did all that for him?") But then, she and Liz had always wanted him to be a real father—nurturing, and all that—which I knew better than to ask. And as for taking responsibility, I was way ahead of where I'd been last June. I'd become a pretty decent cook, I'd figured out how to shop before we ran out of things, and I'd stopped feeling bad about my inability to anticipate the Great Man's wishes after Pris had reminded me that I was his daughter, not his servant.

No, I thought as I watched the shadows of clouds chase each other towards the Bartletts' barns, my life was hardly pitiable. Joan and Rob had no chance of going to college. They worked long hours every day, even weekends, just to make ends meet, and Mrs. Bartlett did, too. All I had to do was keep house and entertain the Great Man's guests. By Vermont standards—heck, by any standards—that was hardly a fate that required support. I squared my shoulders and started hauling the remaining detritus of my Bradley years out of the Skylark's trunk.

Ω

The next morning, I called Green Mountain Stables about my horse—and I was told with marked asperity that no horse had been ordered. Yes, they were sure. Ask my old man.

Thoroughly puzzled, I waylaid the Great Man between Ovid and the piano. "About my horse . . ."

His eyes drifted back from wherever he'd spent the last year and a half. "Horse . . . ah yes. I meant to tell you—the shysters raised the price, and I didn't think it was worth it."

"When was this?"

"April, maybe. Easter."

I'd spent Easter vacation helping Pris, Don, and Debby get ready to move to Texas. Don had made vice president of a big oil company, and despite my negative feelings about oil and capitalism, it was hard to disapprove of their pride in his promotion. "Exactly what did you tell Green Mountain Stables at Easter?"

He smiled benignly. "I told 'em to go to hell."

That explained the asperity. "Was it the horse you objected to, or the price?"

"They wanted three hundred dollars for the summer—outrageous!"

"If I can find a horse for less, that would be okay?"

"Are you sure you want to? Lots of girls your age outgrow—"

"—Not me. You can see things on a horse that you can't see otherwise."

"I suppose that's true," he said reflectively. "Well, see what you can do."

And so it was that my VW Bug's maiden voyage took me to the corrals, lean-to sheds, and shack that together formed the base of Joe the Frenchman. By luck he was there, sitting on a nail keg. I jumped out of the Bug, smiling as widely as the constraints of business allowed.

"Hi, Joe. I've come to see if you might . . .?" I looked at his vacant eyes. "Joe?"

The screen door next to him squeaked open and slammed shut behind a thin woman with one of those faces that could be anywhere between thirty and sixty. "What you want with Joe?" she said, standing in front of him.

"Um . . . I'm Peggy Hamilton, and—"

"Don't matter *what* your name is. Nobody bothers Joe now. —C'mon, Dad." She pulled Joe up by the elbow and propelled him inside.

My errands at the post office and the hardware store gave me time to recover from the shock, so I drove to the Hapneys' barn. Mr. Wolfson walked out the door and tipped his hat. "What kin I do fer you . . . ? Jeesum! Peggy! You got a classy new car!"

"Sure do," I said, smiling as he walked around it appreciatively. "Four on the floor, economical, coolsville. No more Skylarks for me.—Good to see you."

"Same here—you shut of that la-de-da school now?"

"Graduated yesterday. But look—seems my old man canceled my horse."

"Heard about that."

"You *did?*"

He grinned. "Yup. Mr. Green Mountain Stables had a couple too many at Andy's, said quite a bit." The grin faded. "Happen you went to see Joe?"

I nodded. "I wouldn't have, if I'd known . . . What's the score?"

"Wal, his daughter—the one that sees to him now—says it was a stroke, but more likely it was drink. He started downin' a fearful lot after Jake left."

"There wasn't . . . bad news . . . about Jake, was there?"

"Nope—but no news there is the only good news of the winter. Joe in February, then come sugarin' time, Mrs. Hapney drops dead. Embolism, Weller said. Makes 'em go down like a tree—bam!"

"Geez. Poor Sarah."

"She's okay—the money went to her, not her dad. Not this place, though. Seems that's just his, and Weller's worried 'bout he'll be wantin' to make a profit on it now." He shook his head. "But about a hoss. If I recall correctly, someone said there's a lady Westover way, has somethin' she wants to unload. Want me to check that out?"

"Far out! I knew you'd think of something."

"Always glad to help." He watched me get into the Bug. "How's your old man?"

"Still shut down. He's lost without Mother, and nothing I do helps."

He looked at me with an expression I'd never seen in his face before. "Y'know, there's no call fer you to grind yerself down tryin'. He'll git over it in his own way."

"I sure hope so," I said. "But hey, thanks."

Ω

The next Friday brought with it our first weekend guests. I got the beds made and the house tidied, and at a bit after noon I came home with the groceries to find a familiar MG in the driveway.

In the old days, I would have dashed inside to hug Mr. Zander, but instead I sat in the Bug, thinking. I hadn't seen him for almost two years—he'd spent the summer after his Fulbright traveling all over Europe. He'd written me a wonderful letter after Mother died, and another one after Kennedy was shot, but there had been sort of a wall between us after we'd gone driving in the rain that day, even though he'd kept dropping by for tennis and conversation. Or so I'd thought, anyway. Maybe I'd just made it up. Still, I decided to carry two bags of groceries into the house, so hugging would be impossible and he'd see I was earning my keep.

I'd thought too long. When I turned awkwardly from hoisting the two bags out of the VW's back seat, he was there, holding out his arms. "May I help you, madam?"

"Sure," I said, handing him the bags. Ignoring the concern

he quickly masked with a smile, I added, "Glad you're back."

"Glad to *be* back," he said, starting towards the house. I followed at a greater distance than I'd intended, because the bag that held the roast beef and steak tore as I got it out. As I passed the kitchen windows, I heard him say, "Ned—you told me Peggy was doing fine!"

I struggled the bag through the door, wishing he'd put the emphasis on *told* instead of *fine*. "I'll be right back!" I said, easing it down. "Please stay for lunch."

"Yes, do!" said the Great Man, peering into the bags. "Hey, there's no beer!"

"'Don't look at me," I said. "I reminded you this morning that nobody will sell me liquor for another month."

"Oh, yeah," he said vaguely. "Well, Karl, we'll have to make do with tonic or soda."

I went out for the rest of the load, wondering what they were saying about me, but I never found out. Just as we started lunch, Mr. Wolfson stopped by and, at my invitation, stepped into the kitchen, working his hat in his hands. After discussing the weather with the Great Man and Mr. Zander, he turned to me.

"The lady I tole you 'bout is real eager fer you to take her hoss. Says you kin have it free—she jist wants t'git shut of it— and kin you come this afternoon?"

I looked over my shoulder at the Great Man. "How's a free summer horse sound?"

"Fine," he said. "Just don't look it in the mouth." He and Mr. Zander laughed. Mr. Wolfson looked puzzled.

"Why is it free?" I asked.

"She said it bucks, but sounds to me it's jist too much fer her," said Mr. Wolfson. "Comes with tack, an' she'll truck it over here if you want it."

I looked at my watch, then at the Great Man. "Think I have

time to take a look before the Jacksons get here?"

"Go ahead," he said. "Karl and I will get wine and beer."

"Great!" I said, and hurried to the truck with my boots in one hand and my sandwich in the other, feeling a little bad about leaving Mr. Zander so fast.

I felt even worse as we turned off Route 100 on the road that went by Mr. Zander's house, because after a couple of miles it joined up with a road that had been dirt but was now asphalt with a double yellow line down the center. "Geez!" I said. "What's happened?"

"Death in the family," said Mr. Wolfson. "Ol' man Henderson kicked off, left his place to his kids, along with a pile of debts. 'Course, that might jist be the story they put out to make sellin' seem right—"

"—The Hendersons sold? They've been summer folks forever!"

"Forever's got its price on five hundred acres at the base of the Mountain. Fancy big developer coughed up over a million bucks fer it, if you kin b'lieve the stories you pick up at Andy's. Half of it's goin' to condos—see over there?"

I looked. The mowing that Mr. Zander's grandfather had mowed for thirty years had been bulldozed into fake hills with paved roads winding through half-framed buildings; behind it the sugar bush had been "thinned" to make room for more. "Yuk!"

"T'other side of the road," he said, pointing, "is broke up into ten acre lots, goin' fer about what Hapney farm'd fetch. Each, that is."

I was still adjusting to the alien landscape when we pulled up at the Hendersons' house. It was the most handsome place in Westover—huge, white, Victorian—and even with its land gone, it was impressive. A woman rose from its arcaded porch, and as Mr. Wolfson shut off the engine, she walked towards us in a way that somehow made her boots and breeches look feminine. She had to be in her forties, but her curly hair and careful makeup hid it well.

"Isabel Goreson," she said, smiling. "I take it you're my saviors?"

Mr. Wolfson tipped his hat and said he didn't know about that. I held out my hand in Bradley Academy manner. "Peggy Hamilton."

She held my hand an extra second. "Hamilton? Any relation to Edward?"

The question was so familiar I forgot it was unusual in Vermont. "His daughter."

"Goodness!" she said. "I heard he lived near here, and I've been just *dying* to see him again. We met at a conference last winter—I use his translations in *all* my classes."

"He'll be delighted to hear that," I said with practiced neutrality.

"Wonderful," she said. "Well, come see Diamond." She led the way around a corner, revealing a paddock and a bay thoroughbred who trotted to the gate with liquid grace. "There! Isn't he *gorgeous*?"

Mr. Wolfson whistled under his breath. "Where'd you happen across him?"

"Madison Square Garden," she said proudly. "He was a show jumper, but he never finished in the money because bucking between fences in jump-offs added seconds to his times. When I heard his owners were fed up with him, I couldn't resist making them an offer." She laughed. "He seemed so gentle, I was sure he'd teach me how to ride."

Mr. Wolfson's eyebrows shot up. "This ain't a beginner hoss."

"So I found," she said, stroking his face as he stuck it over the fence. "And really, I don't have time to learn. So I'm looking to give him to somebody who'll treat him right."

Mr. Wolfson looked at me. "Wanna give him a try, Peggy?"

I should have said "No, thank you," and left as politely as possible. If there was one certainty in my life, it was that I was never going to *own* a horse. But he was just stunning. "Sure—c'mon, Diamond."

He came along willingly and stood with Olympian tolerance as we tacked him up with Mrs. Goreson's expensive but unoiled saddle. "Thinks the sun shines out his ass," muttered Mr. Wolfson, and added aloud to Mrs. Goreson, "He dumps you?"

"Yeah," she said ruefully. "When we trot. I can't get that up-and-down motion you're supposed to do, and he bucks."

Mr. Wolfson and I exchanged smiles, but as I rode Diamond to the Hendersons' old ring, I realized the mass of power underneath me could send me flying in a second. We started with walks and halts. When we finally trotted, he snorted a bit, but he halted on command. Finally, I asked for a canter and got it with a sizeable hop.

"There!" said Mrs. Goreson. "That's what he does!"

"That's *all*?" I asked as we cantered by her.

"No—it goes on and on if you lose your balance."

I believed her. And I suspected he'd never been ridden outside a ring. Still . . .

"He's great," I said, drawing him up. "But I'll have to talk to my father. I'm supposed to be looking for a summer horse, and I'm not sure any more would be okay."

She smiled. "Suppose I *make* it okay? I'm sure we can work things out."

Man, she was really persuasive. "Let me talk to him and call you this evening."

"Fine," she said.

But when I got home, I found she'd already called. And the Great Man had said yes.

Ω

Diamond arrived in the middle of the Sunday brunch we were sharing with the Jacksons and Mr. Zander, but Mrs. Goreson had read Mr. Jackson's book on Plautus, so it was like old home week. After everybody had watched me unload Diamond and exclaimed at his beauty, Mrs. Jackson—one of those motherly souls who insisted on taking over the household—made extra coffee, and when I finally got back, they were talking Ovid in a way that threatened to continue until dinner time. I slipped in, astonished by the Great Man's animation as he argued, defended translation nuances, and held forth on poetic truth. The whole time Mrs. Jackson and I were washing dishes, the kitchen was full of exciting ideas and discussions, the way it had when I was a kid. As I dried the plates and cups, I reflected sadly that it wasn't just Mother I missed; it was the family she'd made us.

Suddenly Mr. Jackson glanced out the window and jumped up. "My God! Peggy, is your horse loose?"

I was outside before he'd finished the question, but everything was fine. When I'd put Diamond in the pasture, he'd looked around a little, then quietly started cropping grass. But now he'd realized that the enclosure was bigger than a paddock, and as I watched—as everybody gathered outside to watch—he followed the grass track to the tennis court fence at an exploratory, airy trot, turned, then, heading back towards the barn, cantered faster and faster until he broke into a splendid, long-striding gallop.

"Holy Mother!" breathed Mr. Zander. "He's going to jump the gate!"

I watched the way he approached it, shifting his stride, measuring its four-foot height—child's play for a show-jumper—and I started for the barn. But there was no need. Having apparently convinced himself he could do it, he slammed to a stop, whirled, and took off towards the tennis court again.

Mrs. Goreson, who was standing next to the Great Man, looked up at him. "You can see why I was so taken with him! Have you ever seen such a beautiful creature?"

To my surprise, he smiled. "He's certainly lovely to watch."

"Wait until you see Peggy ride him!" she said enthusiastically. "The way she gets him to move is pure poetry!"

She paused, waiting for a proud parental response—then realizing the subject had no interest, she asked him a question about a tricky passage in the closing stanzas of *Metamorphoses*, which drew his attention instantly. As the classicists headed back to the kitchen, I had to admire her perceptiveness.

Mr. Zander stayed outside with me, watching Diamond take a few more runs. "That's almost the definition of joy," he said.

I nodded. "It's probably the first time he's been in a pasture since he was a yearling. Horses of his quality live pretty confined lives."

"Like other people I could mention."

I gave him a withering look. "Even he knows he's inside a fence."

"Sorry. It's just . . . remember what I told you a couple of years ago about Vermont's being the last place you want to be when you're eighteen?"

I shrugged. I wasn't sure my longing to be elsewhere was any less painful for being classic. "College is coming. Bigger fence."

"I wish it were more than that. I know Michigan's Honors College is excellent, and your father is pleased—but I wish you'd looked further afield."

"I did. The further fields turned me down."

His eyebrows rose. "What? You were an honors student—"

"—not at Bradley. Honors students there were girls who took careful notes and parroted them back. I tried that, but what they wanted was . . . well, unimaginative. So I went my own way, and we compromised on comments like 'you're out of your depth, but there are interesting ideas here' and mostly Bs. The school fully expected those Bs to get me into the Seven Sisters, the way they would have ten years ago. But unbeknownst to Bradley, it's not ten years ago, and college admissions have changed. So I'm going to the Honors College, thanking my lucky stars the Great Man talked me into applying."

He looked at me, frowning a bit. "Will you be living at home?"

"Of course."

"Doing the housework? Cooking? Entertaining?"

"Someone's got to do it."

"Not you, necessarily."

"Well, that was the attraction of the further fields. But since it didn't happen we'll work something out. I can manage."

"True. But I hate to see you resigned to—"

"—Can we please, please change the subject?" I turned my head away as laughter drifted out the kitchen window.

I expected him to argue, but Mrs. Goreson called out to him through the screen, so he turned and smiled. "Sure, right there," he said. And added to me, "We'll talk later."

I hoped to God we wouldn't.

Ω

Diamond had a lot to learn about being a trail horse. If there was so much as a log on the path, he tripped over it, an aristocrat faintly puzzled by the idea of an obstacle. On the road, however, he was a tireless ride, and in the barn, he was so sweetly affectionate that sometimes I went out and talked to him. By mid-July, we'd become friends in a way I'd never been with a horse. And he was mine! Every time I groomed or rode him, the prospect of a lifetime partnership laid a bright path through the unspectacular future that lay ahead of me.

One day as we came home, a dark green Cadillac pulled up next to the barn, and Mr. Hapney stuck his head out of its push-button window. "Well, well," he said. "Wolfson *said* you finally had the horse you deserved!" Before I could thank him, he added, "Is your dad at home?"

I glanced at the driveway—the Great Man had taken to going for drives, sometimes for hours. But the Skylark was there, so I said, "Sure. Go in the back door. I'll be right in."

It took me only ten minutes to get to the kitchen, but I sensed that the conversation was nearly over. Hoping to be included, I offered coffee, but Mr. Hapney stood up.

"Well, it's a shame," he said. "It's an excellent investment, you realize."

"That's more in my son-in-law's province than mine," said the Great Man. "And at the moment, he doesn't have the capital. But thanks for stopping by."

It was a dismissal, and though you could see Mr. Hapney wasn't the kind of man who heard dismissals very often, he nodded, smiled at me, and left.

"What was that all about?" I asked.

"He's selling the farm," said the Great Man. "Seems his wife's death has changed his financial situation. Offered it to me as a special deal, he said, for neighbors."

"Selling the farm! And you said no?"

He stubbed out his cigarette ferociously. "I did indeed. You know what his 'special deal' was? A hundred grand! And he only paid thirty-five!"

"But he bought it eight years ago! And he's fixed up the barn and the fences and all the tenant houses! And when Mr. Wolfson and I went to see Diamond, we saw the Hendersons' old farm, divided up into ten-acre lots and going for a hundred grand *each*!"

"You sound like your brother-in-law," he said. It wasn't a compliment.

"All I'm saying," I said, choking back tears, "is that you shouldn't turn down the farm because you think Mr. Hapney's cheating you."

"Maybe not. But I'm certainly not going to spend that kind of money on land that needs constant oversight."

"But if you don't buy it, a developer will snap it up!"

"Developers aren't interested in land this far from the Mountain. Karl's place is in real trouble, but we're perfectly safe."

"That's not—"

"—The answer is *no*. Quite apart from the money, there's too much else going on."

"There is?"

"It would seem so." His changed tone made me look at him quickly, and I caught the awkward look that meant he had to deal with a family problem. "Um," he said, "what would you think of living in a dormitory at the University, instead of living at home?"

Was this a reproach? I swallowed twice before I could bring out, "Why do you ask?"

"Well," he said, fumbling for a cigarette, "Isabel has been working to get me a year-long position as Distinguished Professor of Classics at the University of Virginia, where she teaches. It hasn't come through yet, but she's confident that it will."

Isabel. I drew a blank—then I remembered it was Mrs. Goreson's first name. And I remembered the Great Man's frequent drives. "I see," I said. And I did—not just about the offer, either. But suddenly realizing my response might have sounded churlish, I added, "That's quite an honor! Would you take it?"

"Oh, I think so. It's an excellent department—lots of new people but a long, distinguished tradition. And as Isabel points out, a year away from Michigan and its memories might do me good."

There was no arguing with that. I'd seen for myself how much more cheerful he'd been after those "drives." And he seemed not to be displeased with me at all. "So go for it," I said. "I know all about dormitory life. No problem."

"Good." He smiled awkwardly. "I really want to do right by you, Peggy."

"You do fine!"

"Well, Karl tells me you weren't happy at Bradley." He lit the cigarette he'd been playing with. "Too bad you didn't speak up. I never liked the place, myself. It seemed antiquated even when Pris was there." I stared at him, hardly able to believe what I was hearing. "But you know, your mother was worried about you at the end . . ." He blew a smoke ring, his eyes drifting away as they followed it. After it disappeared, he sat straighter and said, "How about lunch? I'm going out soon, and I'll probably stay through supper. So let's go, huh?"

While I assembled sandwiches, I had an inspiration about the Hapney farm. After the Great Man had taken off, I called Mr. Zander and asked if I could pay him a visit after feeding time—around five o'clock.

Ω

I hadn't been to Mr. Zander's house for two years, maybe even three, since we hadn't gone much of anywhere Mother's last summer. By the time I got there, I realized how right the Great Man had been about the danger it was in: once I'd passed the Hendersons' house, there was a For Sale sign at the base of almost every driveway.

He was standing on his porch, waiting for me with a smile. "Hi, Peggy. You want a drink?"

"Um . . ." What I really wanted was to be ten years old again, so I could run to his arms for comfort. That made it hard to talk. "Actually, I'm here on business."

"Okay," he said neutrally. He led the way into the living room and sat on one of the Morris chairs that stood on either side of his grandfather's oversized mantelpiece. "Shoot."

I sat down in the other chair. "Mr. Hapney's selling his farm. The Great Man won't buy it because he thinks a hundred grand is too much—"

"—Christ! The way land prices are going here, it's the bargain of the century!"

"Right, but see, he also said there was too much going on and he told me . . ." His face told me he knew, so I just said, "about Mrs. Goreson and the Virginia professorship."

He looked uncomfortable. "Still in the works, I think."

"Yeah, but it's about as much of the Real World as he's going to think about right now. He cut me off before I even got to the non-monetary reason to buy Hapney's place: unless somebody interested in farming buys it, Mr. Weller and Mr. Wolfson will have no place to go. Nobody hires men their age, and farming is all they know how to do. And you *know* Mr. Hapney will sell to a developer unless we buy it."

He looked at me sharply. "We? You and your father?"

"No, no—I mean us."

His eyes opened wide. "You and me?"

"Well," I said, suddenly realizing it sounded a little strange, "you. I don't have any money of my own. But if you bought it, I'd run it for you when you were teaching and stuff during the winter."

"Peggy—"

"—Sure, I don't have any experience, but I know *something* about farming, and I'm a quick learner. And of course Mr. Weller and Mr. Wolfson would help me. We'd probably have more horses than cows, but—"

"—Peggy, stop and think. Quite apart from issues of your experience, your education, your writing . . . think of how it would *look*."

"It would look like a farm, not a suburb! That's the point!"

"I'm sure the farm would look just fine. But the situation . . . come on. Even a girl with your straight-laced background must be familiar with the expression 'Sugar Daddy,' and know what your friends Weller and Wolfson think of girls who have them."

I was indeed familiar with the expression; Joe the Frenchman had used it with profane eloquence. I just hadn't . . . I turned redder and redder as I confronted my stupidity. Before I could apologize, though, the phone rang, and he jumped up to answer it.

"Yes?" he said. "Wonderful! No, I'll pass, thanks, but come over for a celebratory drink, won't you? Peggy's here." There was a little silence. "Great. See you soon." He hung up and came back to his chair. "That was your father. The job came through. He and Isabel are on their way to dinner at the Westover Inn, but they're going to stop by here first."

I looked out the window, dimly realizing that what I remembered as a rocky pasture between him and the Mountain was now a perfect green lawn punctuated by three expensive-looking houses. The scene blurred as I thought how naïve I was, trying to stop what was happening to Vermont, to the Great Man, to . . . I stood up. "I think I'll take off."

"Can I persuade you to think again?" he said. "For one thing, they want to include you in their celebration—"

"—Bullshit. They didn't even know I was here!"

"And for another, when you pass them in the driveway, you'll look like a sulky adolescent."

"Okay, okay." I sat down again. "It's just—"

"—hard to take. I know. My mother remarried after my dad died. And after your mother, Isabel is . . . but try to concentrate on how much better he looks." He stood up. "Here they come. I assume we'll say nothing about Hapney farm?"

"Don't rub it in."

He touched my shoulder lightly as he started towards the porch. "Sorry."

Ω

They looked radiant. Or at least, she did. He looked merely pleased, but he was his old, pre-Mother's-cancer self, joking with Mr. Zander about the political machinations that always seemed to accompany honors, and moving into other things I couldn't hear because Mrs. Goreson had taken me aside.

"This will be great for you, too, Peggy," she said, smiling. "You'll get the *real* college experience, instead of living the life of a middle-aged faculty wife. You've been wonderful to your father, but you should be enjoying cruising and the Beatles and going to the movies with your friends."

"I'm okay," I said.

"I'm sure you *feel* okay. But think of the day Diamond arrived and everybody was talking in the kitchen. Instead of joining in, you did the dishes with Jackson's self-deprecating wife. Talk of a model of what a woman has to look out for!"

I bristled, which was strange, because Mrs. Jackson was the very sort of Monday Club woman I'd sworn never to become. "Somebody has to do the dishes."

"Sure, but if you'd waited, we *all* could have done them, and you could have joined the conversation instead of hiding your talents under a domestic bushel. Have you read *The Feminine Mystique?*"

"I've . . . um, heard of it."

"You need to read it, Peggy. 'The new philosophy calls all into doubt'—honest."

"Thank you," I said politely. "I'll see if I can get hold of a copy."

"And look, at the University, get into some women's groups. Girls with upbringings like yours are bound to have trouble transitioning to lives with real opportunities. Meanwhile—" She glanced at the Great Man. "Are we off?"

Mr. Zander's eyebrows rose; he hadn't even offered drinks yet. But the Great Man smiled and turned towards the door. "Sure," he said. Then he stopped, the peculiar "family" expression crossing his face. "Um, weren't you going to tell Peggy about—"

"—Oh yeah," she said, turning to me. "Danforth Academy called me this morning. One of their school horses has gone lame, so they really need Diamond. I fussed, but they have me over a barrel—he's a tremendous tax write-off, and they said it would be no deal if they didn't get a replacement this week. So—"

"—Tax write-off!" I said, feeling myself go cold. "Deal! What do you mean?"

"Omigosh," she said. She turned to the Great Man. "Didn't you *tell* her?"

He shook his head. "You said you would make it clear when you finalized things."

"Oh dear." Mrs. Goreson smiled awkwardly. "Well, Peggy, before I met you, I'd been negotiating with Danforth Academy about donating Diamond to their riding program. They were hesitant because he'd only been ridden by professionals, and they were still considering when you came along. When I called your father, I said that the situation was still up in the air, but that you could have Diamond free until things worked out, which would probably be most of the summer. It seemed like a perfect solution . . . only I somehow thought your father had explained everything, and he thought I had. But neither of us *imagined* we'd let you think Diamond was yours to keep."

I looked from one of them to the other. They weren't lying. They simply hadn't thought to tell me they'd made a deal.

Diamond. Beautiful, affectionate Diamond. Not mine. A school horse, ending up like Emp, sour from too many lessons. I looked down at the floor, willing myself not to cry.

"Um," said Mr. Zander, "Why don't the two of you go celebrate. Peggy and I will talk further."

"Good idea," said the Great Man. To my surprise, he put an arm around my shoulder. "Peggy, I'm sorry about the horse. But the summer's more than half over, and you'll be leaving in late August for orientation anyway. In fact—" he glanced at Mrs. Goreson—"you could go back earlier, if you want. I'll have to rent the house next year, and it's not prepared for tenants. If you wanted to take charge of that, you could live there until the dorms open."

"Go back *now?*"

"If you'd like," he said. "It'd give you something to do—there won't be much for you here with the horse gone."

"That's true," said Mrs. Goreson. "And you could get into the University scene right away."

"Um . . . let me think about it."

"Sure," she said. "Oh, and look—the Danforth Academy trailer will be picking up Diamond at about ten tomorrow."

"Right," I said. "I'll have him all set to go. Have a great time."

"I'm sure we will," said the Great Man. Mrs. Goreson laughed, and the two of them went off to dinner, thick as thieves.

Neither Mr. Zander or I moved until the Skylark drove away.

"Jesus, Peggy," he said finally. "What can I say?"

"Can you tell me—without lying—you didn't know Diamond wasn't mine?"

"I sure can. I'm still trying to take it in. I just assumed . . . Christ."

"It was an accident. They didn't *mean* to leave me out. She just forgot, and he . . . well, without Mother to guide him, he's not long on responsibility." I looked out the window again. "They're well met."

The words fell into a silence that went on and on.

"Well," I said finally. "You won't have to worry about my being Mother to my father any more. They've managed to write me out of their story very neatly. I should look at it as an opportunity to leave Vermont, the way eighteen-year-olds always want to, right?"

"Peggy . . ." He stepped across the space between us and put his arms around me. "Oh, Peggy."

It felt wonderful. It felt safe. But I knew it wasn't. I disengaged myself. "No sugar daddies, remember?"

"God damn," he said, stepping backwards. "Look, I admit I deserve that for introducing the ugly phrase, but—"

"—I asked for it. I realized that a minute too late. What I meant just now was . . ."

"I know what you meant just now. But think. We've been close in a rare and special way since you were seven and I was twenty-seven. Do you really think I'd throw all that over now, when you most need support and affection, just because during those eleven years you've become a beautiful young woman?"

I looked at him, newly aware of how attractive he was, but also of the steadiness with which his eyes met mine. "No," I said finally. "I don't think you would. And it puts you in a very special category. Everybody else I've really loved and admired has died or disappeared. Including Vermont."

"Oh, come, Peggy! Don't exaggerate—"

"—No, I'm serious. I'm sure part of it's being eighteen, but a lot of it's real. It started when Mr. Bartlett died . . . then the baseball games stopped . . . and the tennis court came in . . . and Jake got drafted, and Joe the Frenchman had a stroke. What's left is Joan and Rob, who want to farm and can't afford to, and Mr. Wolfson, who won't have a living after Hapney sells out, and the built-over mowings and pastures of the old Henderson estate, and the For Sale signs on your road . . . everything I loved about Vermont, the whole world I imagined fitting into and loving—it's slipping away."

"'Time and chance happeneth to them all,'" he murmured, looking sadly out the window at the three houses in his view. "Yes, Vermont is changing, and there's not much the Bartletts or Wolfsons—or even the Zanders—of the world can do about the larger economic factors that . . . hey, come sit on the sofa."

I did, and after he'd brought me a box of tissues, we sat side by side until I finally stopped.

"Funny," I said, wiping my face. "I never wanted to be from Michigan, but when I talk about it, I always call it home. Maybe that's where I've belonged all this time."

"Michigan's a good place to be from. But you've been from Vermont in a special way that's shaped your winter life for eleven years. Maybe not the Vermont its natives live in—"

"—You mean it's just something I've invented?"

"On the contrary. It's something's that's nurtured your inventiveness. All those golden summers. All those people in a world so different from your parents'. All those stories. They've always gone back to Michigan with you. And now, you'll be taking all that back with you again, to build on as you construct a life that's finally your own."

"Well," I said, somewhat comforted, "that's true, I guess." Then, after a pause— "Do you think I should take their hint and go back now? Like . . . tomorrow?"

"Maybe not tomorrow," he said dryly, "but as soon as possible. Unless, of course, you want to share the house with them."

"My God!" I said, appalled. "Do you really think they'll . . . ?"

"I do indeed," he said. "Your father, though a brilliant classicist and wonderfully interesting friend, is a man like any other, and Isabel understands that perfectly."

"I . . . see," I said. "Yeah. Okay. Tomorrow I'll clean the barn and pack, but the day after that, I'll go."

"A wise choice. And look, if you need help financially . . ."

"I'm sure that won't be a problem. Whenever the Great Man

feels he hasn't been a very good father, he writes a check."

He laughed, and we both got up.

"So," he said, walking me to the Bug, "day after tomorrow. Come for breakfast."

"You're nuts! I'll be leaving at six."

"Come at five. I'm up at dawn."

"Great, then. Make the coffee super strong. And look—thank you. You've been wonderful."

"You deserve no less," he said. "See you soon."

I drove off, waving. But after I'd passed the Henderson place, I decided to take the short cut over the hill the newly-paved road avoided. It was dirt, and narrow, but the Bug was used to that, and the view from the top was just as beautiful as I'd remembered. I pulled over, got out, and gazed at it in the ethereal evening sunlight. Below me, the white village steeple rose above the roofs of houses and the mowings and pastures beyond them. To my right, a hill rose to the back of the Bartlett's maple grove, still in the glory of its summer green. And beyond that, Rob and Joan, Mr. Wolfson . . .

I slid into the Bug and started it up. But as I followed the road back to the farm I thought I'd love forever and the horse that wasn't mine, my mind was already driving the long-familiar route west across New York, Canada, and the Ambassador Bridge. In just two days, I'd be leaving Vermont, exchanging the past and its embellishments for the future and its promises. It was a wonderful, exciting prospect.

Who would have thought it would hurt so much?

Acknowledgments

"Liar from Vermont" appeared in *The Mind's Eye: The Liberal Arts Journal of Massachusetts College of the Liberal Arts*, 2011.

I am very grateful to the people who supported Peggy's stories as they evolved, particularly to F. D. Reeve, who read the first eight stories in many drafts, to Beth Kanell, who encouraged me in dark and doubtful moments, and to Katharine O'Connell, whose invaluable suggestions saved me from many embarrassing errors.

Neil Raphel and Janis Raye committed themselves to Peggy when she was seven and awaited her maturity with patient enthusiasm, while Adrienne Raphel's incisive readings helped define the trajectory of Peggy's career.

48625737R00110

Made in the USA
Lexington, KY
07 January 2016